Paint
by
Magic

KATHRYN REISS

Paint by Magic

HARCOURT, INC.

Orlando   Austin   New York   San Diego   Toronto   London

Requests for permission to make copies of any part of the work
should be mailed to the following address: Permissions Department,
Harcourt, Inc., 6277 Sea Harbor Drive, Orlando, Florida 32887-6777.

www.HarcourtBooks.com

First Harcourt paperback edition 2003

The Library of Congress has cataloged the hardcover edition as follows:
Reiss, Kathryn.
Paint by magic: a time travel mystery/Kathryn Reiss.
p. cm.
Summary: After his mom suddenly starts acting old-fashioned,
eleven-year-old Connor is transported back to 1926, where
he must discover and break the mysterious hold an obsessed artist
has on his mom that is trapping her between times.
[1. Time travel—Fiction.] I. Title.
PZ7.R2776Pai 2002
[Fic]—dc21 2001005659
ISBN 0-15-216361-1
ISBN 0-15-204925-8 pb

Text set in Sabon
Display set in Gasteur
Designed by Cathy Riggs

A C E G H F D B

Printed in the United States of America

FOR BERNHARD KOCH

What is time?
A mystery, a figment—and all-powerful.
—THOMAS MANN, *The Magic Mountain*

Acknowledgments

Enthusiastic thanks, again, to Tom Strychacz, my husband, for his many careful readings, clever ideas, and constant support.

Thanks, also, to Karen Grove, my editor at Harcourt, for her amazing fine-tuning capabilities, and to Jean Weishan at Mills College, for her computer skills.

This story could not be told without all of you.

Paint
by
Magic

PART ONE

Black Magic

That's my last Duchess painted on the wall,
Looking as if she were alive...
— ROBERT BROWNING,
My Last Duchess

Padua, Italy. April 1479

Lorenzo da Padova unscrewed the cap of his dagger to reveal the secret hiding place. He tipped some of the powdered poison into a small bowl. Once the cap was screwed back into place, it was impossible to detect that the dagger was anything other than what it appeared—a short, exceedingly sharp weapon.

Now he was ready to paint his masterpiece. *This* would be the painting that would secure his fortune and favor with his patrons. *This* would earn his work a place in the greatest palazzi, perhaps in the king's own palace! He was not yet thirty; he was in the prime of his life; he was ready for fame. *This* was why he had abandoned his silly wife and mewling children. He was meant for greater things. His name would be famous—it would last throughout history!

It *must*. He would do anything to see that it did.

Lorenzo opened his wooden paint box and pulled out pouches of pigment. His servant had brought the wooden pail of eggs—fresh this morning. Lorenzo reached into the pail and selected one, inspecting it for cracks or imperfections. Nothing must sully the luster of his paints. His lips twitched as he worked. He broke the egg deftly and separated the yolk, using the tip of his dagger to mix it with the powder in the small bowl. Then he untied the first pouch and sprinkled in the pigment. In his excitement his hand shook and some of the colored dust sifted down to the floor.

Lorenzo cursed under his breath: *Diàvolo!* He mixed in the rest of the powder with more care. The contents of the bowl turned a beautiful cobalt blue.

After the first bowl of paint was ready, he prepared the others, using an egg for each, his special powder from the dagger, and the pigment. Deepest orange. Sea green. Two different yellows—one the pale sunshine of butter, the other a deep golden. Purple like the setting sun. Each color was perfect.

As he worked, his smile played about his lips. This unwavering smile was well known among his fellow painters. It was deceptively sweet at first glance, but it couldn't mask the essential coldness, the hardness of

Lorenzo. They called him Il Sorridente—the Smiler. His smile held a hint of unspeakable evil.

Lorenzo mixed his paints as he waited for his lovely model to arrive. He mixed brown—like the firewood his servants stacked in the kitchens. Silvery gray—like the tankard that held his ale. Red—like the crimson cushion on the model's stool. He chuckled as he mixed the last color, thinking about his soon-to-be-painted masterpiece, and about the young model who would make it all possible. The last color he mixed was black.

Black—like his own evil heart.

∽ Chapter 1 ∽

What's Wrong with This Picture?

*T*here was no mistaking it. Something was wrong. It was like when you look at one of those what's-wrong-with-this-picture puzzles. You know something is weird—but what? Then you look a little longer and you start to see stuff you hadn't noticed before, like a dagger hiding in a tree. Or a face in the shadows on a mountain.

Weirder still if you find your own *mom* staring out of the picture.

That's what happened to me. More or less. I was coming home from school one day last fall, a whole two hours earlier than usual because my after-school computer class had been cancelled at the last second when the teacher got sick. It felt strange to be taking the early bus, knowing there'd be time just to hang out on my own. I was making plans, like how I'd bring a whole bag of chips and a huge bowl of salsa up to my room and watch TV. Or how I could watch my *Star Wars* videos for the fiftieth time. It was going to be so cool to be in the house with time to myself. For once.

So when I let myself into the front hall with my own key and heard a noise coming from the living room, I froze. It was our housekeeper Mrs. White's day off, and no one else should have been home yet. For a second I was worried about burglars, but when I peeked across the hall, there was my mom—of all people—sitting on the living-room couch. She was just sitting there with a big book open on her lap, looking up with a little smile, as if she'd heard me come in and was glad to see me. And for some crazy reason she was holding a long-stemmed red rose in one hand.

"Hey, Mom," I said, shrugging out of my jacket. "What's with the rose?"

Her smile stayed just the same, and she didn't move at all. It was as if she were a statue or something. I dropped my jacket onto the floor and entered the living room. "Mom, are you okay? You look different—are you sick?"

My mom commutes to Oakland and doesn't usually get home until late, sometimes not till I'm in bed. And she's never sick. She says she doesn't have time to be sick, what with her job and her clients and all the work she has to do being a hotshot lawyer. She's a partner in the firm of Johnson, Judd, Jones, and Rigoletti. Mom's the Rigoletti part. As always, she stands out in a crowd.

"Mom?" She didn't answer me. It was as if she didn't even hear me or see me—though her eyes were wide open. Then I noticed that she wasn't blinking. She was just holding the big book—but she wasn't reading it—and that rose in her hand stayed perfectly motionless. It was very freaky.

I reached out hesitantly and touched her shoulder, feeling the soft, lacy sleeve of the swirly dress I'd never seen before. *Not* her usual style.

"Connor!" she shrieked, suddenly coming to life and snapping the book shut like a trap. I jumped back, like she'd turned into a tiger.

Then she was up off the couch and grabbing me in a humongous hug. The book slid to the floor with a thunk. "Connor, darling! My baby! My little boy! Let me look at you—oh, my goodness, you are absolutely the cat's meow—you haven't changed a bit!" The rose tickled my ear.

She must be *very* sick. "*Whoa,* Mom. It's been, like, *one* day since you saw me last time." I tried to pull out of her arms—we're not a very huggy-kissy family, after all—but she held on like a big bear. This was sort of scaring me.

"I can't believe it." She smoothed her hand over my blond hair. "My own, sweet, curly Connor."

"Yuck, Mom. Lay off!" I pulled back, scowling at her.

It was strange how she looked so different from yesterday. It wasn't just the new haircut—short and curled into little waves that bobbed on her cheeks—and her new clothes, but she smelled different, too. Like fresh flowers—not her usual spicy perfume.

She let me go. "Sorry, love. I'm just—just so glad to see you." Her voice was trembly and her eyes were tearful.

She kept sneaking little looks at me. Then she laughed and ruffled my hair. "But don't look so worried, Con. I'm here now. I'm back."

I gave her a look. "Okay, Mom, whatever you say."

"Connor Rigoletti-Chase." Mom pronounced my name slowly, as if savoring the sound.

I frowned. "Whatever." I hardly ever use our double-barrelled last name. Just Chase. It's easier.

"Come to the kitchen, darling." Mom reached for my hand. "Growing boys need their afternoon snacks—and I've got something in the oven you're going to love."

Oven? When had my mom learned to cook?

She picked up my jacket and the fallen rose petals, and carried them out of the living room. I just stood there for a moment, feeling the strangeness. Somehow even with my mom out of the room, the living room still felt...different. As if something had happened there. I leaned down and picked up the big book she'd been reading.

It was one of the books that usually lies on the coffee table, in the living room, with a lot of other big books, the kind no one ever reads. No one is even *meant* to read these books—they're just the ones the decorator told my parents were needed on the table to give the room a cozy and lived-in yet sophisticated and elegant air—though hardly anyone ever uses the room, anyway. The decorator found the books in an antique store and thought they had the right "look" for our coffee table. I put the big book back on the table. It was called *Cotton in the*

Twentieth Century, probably about weaving or sewing or something. It looked dead boring.

"Connor!" Mom's voice was shrill. She stood in the living-room doorway. "Leave that silly book alone and come get your snack."

I followed her to the kitchen. It was strange to see Mom working in the kitchen instead of Mrs. White or Ashleigh. Ashleigh is our baby-sitter. She lives in the apartment over our garage and takes care of my sister, Crystal, and me when she's not doing whatever people in college do. She's been with us for nearly four years, ever since our au pair from Switzerland left, and my parents have said a million times they have nightmares about the day Ashleigh will graduate and leave us.

Mom turned to me with a swirl of her skirt. "Crystal should be home by now, shouldn't she, Connor?"

"Nah," I told her. "It's not nearly time. She gets here closer to six."

Mom pursed her lips. "That seems so late for a child to be getting home."

"Well, you're the one who signed us up for our activities." *Duh,* I thought. As if Mom didn't know! She and Dad paid megabucks for all our extra lessons and stuff.

Crystal is my thirteen-year-old sister, and usually the less said about *her,* the better. But right now I would have been happy to see her home on an early bus. She might know what had happened to Mom's clothes, for one thing.

Mom's soft blue dress had a knee-length skirt with little glittery glass bead things sewn into it. She looked sparkly, like somebody in an old-time movie. Usually she wore elegant, businesslike clothes in gray or beige, with colorful silk scarves around her neck. She looked younger today, somehow, in the blue dress—younger even than she does on weekends, with her pale hair in a ponytail, rushing around, driving me to karate, Crystal to ballet, and both of us to soccer and gymnastics.

Mom kept smiling like she was so thrilled to see me as she led me to the kitchen table. "Now, sit yourself right down and tell me about yourself. I mean, about your day."

"The computer teacher threw up so they cancelled class, and I caught the early bus home."

"Oh, dear. Nothing serious, I hope," Mom said. She put two plates on the table, one for me and one for her, and two glasses. "Now, go ahead. Sit down. Why are you looking so anxious, honey? Aren't you hungry?"

"Sure, I'm hungry," I said agreeably, and sat down. I'm always hungry, but I felt antsy. I'm used to getting my *own* snack after school. But more than that, it was hard to relax when everything seemed somehow *changed*.

One change was that my snack didn't come out of the freezer, where all my microwave kid-meal snacks are stored. Instead Mom thrust her hands into oven gloves and opened the oven door. She brought out a cake pan filled with something fresh and smelling like heaven. "Cool!" I said.

"It's hot, actually," Mom said, then smiled, "so don't burn your mouth." She poured me a big glass of milk and tipped the cake out onto a plate. "Drink up," she said cheerfully. "We'll have to wait a few minutes to cut the cake. But you can have seconds if you want. Twelve-year-old boys have hollow legs."

"Eleven, Mom. I'm eleven." I paused. "And can't I have Coke instead of milk?"

She flushed. "Silly me—of course you're still eleven! But—no Coke. Milk is better for young bones."

I drank the milk without a word, and when she served me the cake, I ate four pieces. No way was I going to remind her that she and Dad had been talking only last week about how they were going to sign Crystal and me up for a fitness sports camp to keep us in shape over the long summer vacation—as if we don't spend the whole school year doing *activities* already! I just wanted to spend the summer being a couch potato. I mean, who wouldn't?

Anyway, the cake seemed to melt in my mouth. I decided I could get used to coming home from school to my mom and homemade snacks every day.

As I savored each bite of this unexpected treat, I reached behind me to the cookbook shelf, where we keep the remote for the kitchen TV, but it wasn't there. Then I looked over to the counter where the little TV usually sat, and it wasn't there, either. "Hey," I called. "Mom! I think we've been robbed!"

Mom was at the sink, peeling potatoes. *Peeling potatoes?* I'd never seen her do that in my life. "No, darling, we haven't been robbed. I just thought a break from TV would do us all some good." Instead of stuffing the potato peelings down the disposal the way Mrs. White does, Mom collected them into a bowl and set them aside. "We'll have to start a compost pile," she said with a little smile. "'Waste not, want not.'"

It was all very, very weird. *"Whatever."*

"You know, dear," she said gently, "years ago kids didn't have TV and they found plenty to do. You will, too; wait and see."

"But, Mom! What about my shows?" I *always* watch TV after school!

I stomped out of the room, ignoring Mom when she called for me to come back and rinse my plate. *Rinse my plate?* That was Mrs. White's job. Or Ashleigh's. I would just watch my shows in the family room.

But when I looked into the family room, the big-screen TV wasn't there, either. The wall looked blank without it. I tore upstairs to my room. The TV on my dresser was gone, too!

I went crazy. I ran through all the rooms—my sister's, my parents', the guest room—all the TVs were gone! I ran downstairs and out the door, to the garage, then up the narrow steps in the garage to Ashleigh's apartment. I knocked, but when there was no answer, I barged right in. Ashleigh never locks her door. I'm not usually a snoop (except when I'm spying on Crystal), but I just had to see whether Mom had tossed out Ashleigh's TV, too.

No, there it was, complete with VCR and Nintendo.

I plopped down in relief and reached for the remote. Bliss.

Bliss for about three minutes—because there was Mom again, peering in Ashleigh's front door like the vice police or something. "Oh, Connor," she said sorrowfully. "Con, honey, come down with me and I'll read to you."

"*Read* to me?" I must have shrieked without knowing it, because Mom put her finger to her lips. "I hate to read, and I'm missing my shows! Now, leave me alone and—"

"*Shh.* That's enough. I don't want you coming in here without Ashleigh's permission."

"I don't, usually, but I want to watch—"

"No. I want to see what else you can find to do. Go over to Doug's."

"Doug has choir after school today," I snapped.

"Well, go out and play."

Play? Was she kidding?

Apparently not. She turned off the TV and hustled me out of Ashleigh's apartment, down the stairs into the garage, and then back into our house. "You can play in the backyard, or ride your bike, or climb a tree—"

"Mom, we don't *have* any trees." That was all I could think to say. Though it was true. My dad told me there had once been a whole lemon grove where our housing development now stood, but a big fire fifty years ago had burned almost everything down, and the rest had been bulldozed later to build the new houses. Our yard was covered with thick green grass, with flower beds along the redwood fence separating it from Doug's yard next door. Our grass and flowers were tended by an ancient guy named Gregorio, the weekly gardener. In one corner our old blue-and-orange plastic climbing structure still stood, with a swing and a slide and a lookout tower. Did she expect me to *play* on that?

"You'll think of something to do," Mom said. There was a steely expression in her eyes as she turned and went back to the kitchen.

Instead of going outside to *play*, I stomped up to my bedroom. It was a cool room, basically, though I think maybe the decorator my parents hired went a *little* bit overboard with the *Star Wars* theme. I love *Star Wars*, don't get me wrong, and I love the dark blue and gold star wallpaper and the constellations stuck up on the ceiling in glow-in-the-dark plastic. And the furniture is totally cool, too. My bed is a plastic model of a starship, and there's a trundle bed that looks like a booster rocket underneath that can be pulled out for a guest.

My dresser looks like a robot, with the different drawers pulling out from the robot's body. My TV used to be on top.

The desk takes up the whole wall with the window, and it's like a big command center with my computer and telephone and my music system. I hurried over to the desk command center now, so I could call my dad in San Francisco, where people pay him big bucks to do things with computers. He always said not to call him at work unless it was an emergency, but I figured this was an emergency. He needed to know that Mom had thrown away our TVs. How was he going to watch *his* shows?

I reached for the phone—but things were more serious than I'd thought. The TVs weren't the only things Mom had tossed. My phone was gone! And the computer—you guessed it. When I tried to turn it on, nothing happened. My light worked okay, and my CD player worked, so I knew we weren't in the middle of a blackout or something. Mom had removed all of the cables!

I stormed down the stairs to confront my mom—but at the living-room door, I stopped short.

There she sat, just like before, looking cool and unruffled in her light blue dress, with the big antique book open on her lap. There was a saucer on the table next to her, and a plate with a slice of cake. She held her teacup as if about to take a drink, but she wasn't drinking. She was just sitting there like a statue—and her face was frozen in a look of pure terror.

"Mom?" I said. Suddenly I felt scared. The air grew colder, and there was a strange silence all through the house—especially in that room, blanketing my mom. She didn't even notice I was there.

"Is that the book you wanted to read to me?" I demanded loudly from the doorway.

She jumped, slapping the book shut. The tea sloshed onto the couch. When she looked up at me, there was a bewildered expression in her eyes, but the scared look was gone. "Book?" she said. "Oh! Not at all—this is another book entirely."

"Are you all right, Mom?" My moment of being scared was over—but things still felt weird.

"Of course," she said in a firm voice, as if speaking firmly would make it true. "Let's go to the family room and I'll be happy to read something to you, darling."

"No thanks. I'm going outside to *play*."

Our street—Lemon Street—ended in a cul-de-sac, a dead-end circle like most of the streets in our development, except the one leading out to East Main, past Kmart and the grocery store, then on to the maze of freeways. Our school is on the other side of the freeway tangle, and sometimes the school bus sits in traffic for twenty minutes just trying to inch past all the commuters. We could practically *walk* faster—but who walks, anyway?

I sat on the front step, looking out at the empty road. I don't think I'd ever sat there before, and I'd lived here for eleven years—ever since I was born. But better out here than inside with Mom and her weirdness.

I sighed. No sign of life, except for the dog across the street, who barked at me sharply from his fenced-in front yard. He was excited—glad to see me. Probably his days were really boring, just looking out at the street, with nothing to guard or chase, and no company. Nobody's really home on our street till evening because all the adults work and the kids are at school or day care. It would be a good street to come to if you were a burglar, except that all the houses, including ours, have Silent Sentry alarm systems hooked up.

I guessed I could ride my bike—but where to? I looked up at big old Mount Diablo rising above our town. There's no more "grove" in Shady Grove, but the shade's still there, and always will be, when the late afternoon sun hits the mountain. It was shady out here now, and growing dark. Not exactly great for *playing*.

I checked my watch. It was almost five-thirty. Crystal would be home soon. So I figured I would just wait for my sister's bus. Can you believe it? First time I ever *wanted* to see her. But she had to be warned that something very, very weird was going on with Mom.

∽ Chapter 2 ∽

The Statue

I sat there listening to the barking dog until the yellow school bus stopped at the corner of our street. Then I got up and walked down to meet Crystal. She was the only one getting off at our stop. She waved to somebody still on the bus and sauntered along in a jaunty sort of way, her blond ponytail bouncing, until the bus drove away. Then she slowed down and stopped smiling. Her footsteps seemed to drag even more when she saw me coming toward her. Obviously she was as thrilled to see me as I usually am to see her.

It's not like I hate my sister or anything. She's not especially mean to me, not the way Doug's little sister, Becca, is to him—always rampaging through his room and messing with his stuff. Crystal is in seventh grade and has a few good friends, but otherwise she keeps to herself pretty much. She looks a lot like Mom, tall and thin, with the same yellowish hair (Crystal likes to call it *golden*). She's very private and is always ordering me to stay out of her room. Once Doug and I hid under her bed after we got home from school, and no one even knew we were in the house. Crystal was messing around in her room, putting on makeup and stuff, and we spied on her. When Ashleigh called that it was time for dinner, Doug and I reached out and grabbed Crystal's ankles. You should have heard the screams. I'm surprised they didn't set off the burglar alarm.

Crystal's bed looks like a castle, with a headboard made of some sort of fake stone built like a turret. There's a pink flag coming out the top, and a painted Rapunzel with a long yellow braid hanging from the top window. Her desk chair is a velvet padded golden throne, no kidding. She's not into fairy tales, like you might think, but is really big on modern-day royalty. She's got this thing for kings and queens and stuff. Her goal is to go to England and meet everybody, and it would be like she was already friends with them because she's read all these books about them. She plans to marry Prince William or Prince Harry. Prince William is supposed to be king someday, so that would make Crystal the queen, and she's already planning how to decorate their palace. If it falls through with William or Harry, she's got plans to hook me up with some English princesses named Beatrice and Eugenie. I told her I'd only ever marry somebody whose name I could pronounce.

Anyway, Crystal was walking slower and slower and finally stopped in front of me. "What are *you* doing here?" she asked, as if I were the last person in the world she'd expect to see on Lemon Street.

"I've come to warn you about Mom," I began.

"She's home from work early, and something's wrong with her. She keeps freezing up—like she's in a trance."

"Is she sick?" Crystal asked quickly, and started walking fast. "Is it, like, a brain tumor?" Ever since our grandmother died last year of cancer, Crystal has been worried that something will happen to one of our parents. And now something had, but not like Crystal meant.

"She's not sick," I assured her, "but she's sort of gone crazy. She looks different, for one thing, and she's acting like she hasn't seen me in a year—for another thing. *And* she's gotten rid of all the TVs—"

"*What?*" shrieked Crystal, latching on immediately to the most important part.

"Yup. Every TV in the whole house."

"But there's a special on about Prince Charles tonight! And after that, I need to watch—"

"Well, you won't be watching anything. She'll probably send you out to *play,* just like she did me."

Crystal stopped again and stared at me. "What do you mean, *play?*" We were in front of our house now. The dog across the street barked once more, then fell silent.

A cold wind was blowing. It blew a sheet of old, yellowing newspaper down our quiet, empty street. You could hardly see Mount Diablo anymore, the sky was so dark. "Let's go inside," I said, and sighed. "Then you can see for yourself."

We went in. Mom was standing at the kitchen counter, with a big knife in her hand. Sliced tomatoes lay on the cutting board, and something was simmering on the stove.

It smelled wonderful—almost as good as the Thanksgiving feast we'd had at our favorite restaurant downtown. And it sure smelled a lot better than our usual microwaved Reddi-Meals.

Mom's hand held the knife steady over the tomatoes. Steady and unmoving. A gentle smile was locked on her face, but her eyes looked panicked. She must have cut herself somehow. There were little beads of blood at her hairline. One slid slowly down the side of her face and dripped onto the counter.

"Mom!" I shouted.

No response. Mom was a statue of a lady cooking dinner. I felt a flutter of panic in my stomach, like a little moth trapped at a closed window, and I heard Crystal's sharp intake of breath just behind me. Then I stepped right up close to Mom and clapped my hands hard.

"Yo, Mom! Earth to Mom!" I yelled. That did the trick. Mom sort of shivered for a second, and the knife dropped out of her fingers. I saw her take a deep breath. Then she turned to us, her empty eyes filling with pleasure after a moment.

"Oh!" she cried, delight in her voice. "Crystal, darling!" She hugged my sister. "It's wonderful to see you! You look just lovely! Just the way I remember you!" She dashed away the blood from her forehead, looked startled at the bright red stain on her finger, then wiped it on her apron.

"Mom—how did you hurt yourself?" I demanded.

"I'm not hurt at all. I'm fine," Mom said in a cheerful voice. "I'm the bee's knees!"

Crystal looked worried. "Um—*bee's knees,* Mom? You were bleeding. And you look *different.* Your hair is totally retro—and what's with the dress? Looks like Goodwill."

"I guess I'm in my flapper phase," Mom said with a tender little smile. She smoothed her hair. "The haircut is called a bob, darling. And it would suit you, too."

"No thanks, Mom."

"Anyway, come and sit down and tell me about your day while you eat your snack. I've saved you some cake."

There on the table was a tall glass of milk and a generous slice of pound cake. Crystal shook her head.

"I'll get fat if I eat that! I'll just have a diet Coke."

Mom pulled Crystal to the table. "Now, one little piece of cake won't make you fat or spoil your supper, and milk is much better for a growing girl's bones than soda pop. So just sit down and enjoy."

Crystal gave me a look, but she sat and sipped the milk. She glanced at the counter where the kitchen TV used to be. "So, Mom," she began conversationally, "Con tells me you've junked our TVs."

Mom beamed at her. "Let's just say I've removed them."

"But they'll be back, right? Like, soon? Like, in time for me to watch 'Prince Charles, Man for All Seasons' tonight at eight?" She glanced at the wall clock. "I'm already missing the rerun of *Cheers*!"

"No, honey. It's time for us all to do other things. Get to know each other again. Read some books. Play—"

"Connor is right! You *have* gone crazy!"

Mom walked serenely over to the stove, where some onions in a frying pan accounted for the good smell in the kitchen. She stirred the onions, shook in some spices from a little jar, and added the freshly chopped tomatoes from the cutting board. It was as if she were in a world of her own. And Crystal and I couldn't ruffle her.

"Come with me," I whispered to Crystal. She abandoned her snack and followed me silently out of the room. First I took her upstairs to show her that my TV and phone were gone, and my computer disconnected. Then we checked in her room and found the same. She clutched herself around the middle and groaned as if she were dying.

"I can't believe her!" she kept saying over and over.

I showed her that the guest room TV and our parents' bedroom TV were also gone. Luckily, we discovered that the phone in our parents' room was still there on the table next to the bed. "Quick!" I said. "Let's call Dad. Maybe he'll know what to do about Mom."

But Crystal glanced at the bedside alarm clock and shook her head. "He'll be in a meeting now, or at the club for his workout. We'll have to wait and talk to him when he gets here."

"Ashleigh's TV is still in her apartment," I said. "Maybe she'll let you come over tonight and watch your show."

"Maybe." Crystal brightened for a second. But only for a second. "I just wish I knew what's made Mom do this." She sighed. "Mom seemed perfectly normal when we left for school this morning, didn't she? No, wait— we didn't see her this morning, did we?"

I shook my head. "No, Ashleigh made breakfast." Such as it was. Breakfast wasn't really a meal in our house. But Ashleigh had been here this morning, putting Blueberry Twirls into the toaster and handing them to us on our way out the door. We hadn't seen our parents. Mom and Dad had probably both left before we woke up.

"Well, Mom was fine last night, then," insisted Crystal. She fingered a tendril of her long pale hair. "Wasn't she?"

I tried to remember. Last night seemed so long ago— back when everything was normal. Ashleigh had given us macaroni and cheese for dinner while we watched the news and a talk show—I couldn't remember which one—and then I'd gone up to my room. I phoned Doug to ask about the math homework, and then I did my work sheets in front of the TV. The show was some kind of emergency-room drama, kind of gory with all sorts of severed body parts, but it went well with fractions. Later, after Ashleigh called upstairs to say good night, I put on my headphones and drifted off to sleep to a *Star Wars* story tape. Lots of times when I do that, I dream about *Star Wars*.

"You know what?" I said. "I don't think we saw Mom and Dad last night, either. It couldn't have been too long ago, though, because otherwise we'd have missed them."

"Well, yeah," she agreed slowly. "It's not like they've been out of town or anything."

"But Mom was here when I got home, just sitting in the living room, looking at that book—" I stopped, remembering how Mom had snapped the book shut.

"What book?" demanded Crystal.

I jumped up off our parents' king-sized bed. "Come with me!"

We ran downstairs, peering around corners like spies to make sure Mom didn't see us. I'm not sure why I didn't want her to know we were going to look at the old book. But I was glad to see she was still cooking stuff in the kitchen. It sure smelled good—even better than macaroni and cheese from a box.

The book lay on the coffee table in the living room, just where Mom had left it. It was closed, but I saw that the jacket flap was marking a page—probably the one she had been studying so intently.

"*Cotton in the Twentieth Century,*" read Crystal. "Cotton? What's she reading about cotton for?" She picked up the heavy book and sat down with it on her knees. "I never even knew we had this book."

"The decorator brought it," I said dismissively. "Like all the other ones." The decorator had told my mother it was part of the house's "total look."

Crystal flipped open the Cotton book and glanced at the jacket flap. "It's an *art* book," she said. "Cotton is a painter. An artist."

I sat down next to her and looked. It said that

Fitzgerald Cotton had been born right here in Shady Grove in 1883. It said he had captured the early decades of the twentieth century in his exquisite and luminous paintings of family and home. It said he was distantly related to an Italian artist from the fifteenth century.

I didn't know Mom was interested in paintings. The ones she and Dad bought at the decorator's suggestion were kind of wild-looking abstract prints, all bright colors and odd shapes. But the paintings in this book weren't abstract at all. They looked almost like photographs. Crystal and I stared at the page marked by the jacket flap. We both frowned down at it, puzzled.

I don't know what I'd expected. Something that might inspire Mom's weirdness? Pictures of a dragon destroying television sets with huge bursts of flame? Or something really psychedelic, like those pictures made of colored dots that you stare at until something shifts in your brain and suddenly you see it's really a kangaroo or a flying saucer or something.

But this was a perfectly ordinary painting of a family sitting at a dinner table. There were a grandfather and a grandmother standing up, and the grandmother was just putting down a big silver tray with a cake in the middle of it. The cake was a birthday cake—with nine candles lit—probably for the little girl sitting with a stack of presents in front of her, the one with her hair cut like a helmet, topped with a humongous pink bow. There were a bunch of kids and grown-ups sitting around the table together waiting for that birthday cake. You could just see their heads along the sides of the painting. The caption under the picture said ELSIE'S PARTY, 1926.

It was kind of cool how the painter—that Fitzgerald Cotton guy—had made it look like the woman was just about to set the cake down but hadn't *quite* done it. Maybe that's what made it seem almost like a photo. Caught in the act.

The stuff on the table looked pretty ordinary. Empty dishes and silverware and glasses of water showed that supper had already been eaten and the cake was the dessert. There was a glass dish with little candies in it, and a bowl of whipped cream. A bowl of grapes or something, too. All very real looking and painted well, if you like that sort of thing. But nothing special, at least nothing I could see—

Until then I *did* see.

And so did Crystal.

There was a woman sitting on the right side of the table. A woman with golden hair curled in careful waves along her cheeks, and a big, excited smile as she leaned across the table to talk to somebody sitting on the other side. She wore a yellow dress—in a style that we recognized, just as we recognized that face, that smile. The woman in this picture painted years before she was born looked exactly like our mom.

I flipped through the pages, disbelief like a strong current pulsing through me—disbelief mixed with excitement, and something else, too.

Fear.

Because there were more pictures of Mom—pictures I recognized. Mom on an unfamiliar couch, with a book on her lap, holding a rose. Mom in somebody else's kitchen, chopping tomatoes.

"Crys—" I whispered, my heart hammering.

"I see them," she whispered back.

And then there was Mom in person, walking into the living room with a vase of freshly arranged flowers. She set the vase on the coffee table and turned to us—and her smile went cold when she saw what we were doing.

"Crystal! Connor! Give me that book this instant."

"*Whoa,* Mom!" I said, standing up quickly. "We were just looking at it—and anyway, how come—" I'd been about to ask her about the woman in the paintings, but something made me stop.

"It's mine," Mom said, her voice as cold as her smile.

"Like, haven't you ever heard of *sharing*?" asked Crystal haughtily, slamming the book shut. "What are you screaming at us for? What did we do?" But her voice trembled.

Mom snatched up the heavy book and held it to her chest as if it were a protective shield. Two bright patches of red stood out on her cheeks like splotches of paint. "Mind your manners," she told us in an icy tone of voice I'd never heard from her before. "And do not lay a finger on this book again. Do you hear me?"

Silence stretched out around us as Mom and Crystal held a staring contest. It got so quiet and so tense I thought I could hear Doug in his room next door, zapping creatures at his PlayStation.

But the noise was at our own front door. We all jumped when we heard a heavy footstep in the hallway.

"It's okay!" hissed Crystal. "Dad's home early!"

"Thank you, thank you, thank you," I whispered to whatever cancelled meeting had sent him home to save us.

∾ *Chapter 3* ∾

Cold Turkey

I was so relieved to see my dad home early that I tore into the front hall, barrelled right into him, and wrapped my arms around his chest. He's big and solid and still looks like the football star he was in college, thanks to his daily workouts at his office fitness center. Laughing in a kind of baffled way, he hugged me back. We don't hug very much in my family, but with Mom being so weird, I needed a hug.

"Well, hi, Con," Dad said to me. "How's it going?"

"Dad!" I cried. "You're home! You're home!" I was hanging on Dad like he could save me from drowning or something.

"Oh, Dad!" Crystal ran to clutch his arm. Between the two of us, he was having trouble taking off his coat. "I'm so glad you're here. You'll never believe—"

"Hey, you two!" laughed Dad, juggling us. "Where's the fire?"

"Grant, darling," Mom said, coming into the hall.

Crystal and I let go of Dad and backed off. "I've missed you so much." She stood on tiptoe to kiss his cheek. Dad looked stunned. He and Mom never acted mushy together. In fact, they used to bicker and argue a lot, but lately they'd hardly been home at the same time. And when they were, they sort of ignored each other. I didn't think I'd really heard them talking together for weeks.

"Hey, Pam," Dad said, still looking sort of bewildered but pleased at her kiss. "I got your message to come home early, so here I am. But what's going on?" He scanned our faces. "Kids? What's wrong?"

"I just couldn't wait to see you again," Mom said in a soft voice. "After all this time."

We were standing there like robots, sort of stiff. How could I tell Dad about all the weirdness with Mom right there in the hall with us? But then again, he could see for himself she wasn't acting normal.

"'All this time'?" he asked, puzzled. "All this whole, long day, Pam?"

"Oh, it's been a very, very long day, Grant," said Mom with a little hiccoughy laugh. "You have no idea."

"Listen, Dad!" Crystal butted in. "It's a good thing you're home early. Connor and I were going to call you—you've always said we could if there's an emergency. And there *is* an emergency, Dad!"

I glanced nervously over at Mom, and she was frowning at us. That made me even more nervous.

"You have to talk to Mom!" Crystal's voice rose. "Talk some sense into her so I get my TV back—or any one of the TVs she's thrown away—in time to watch my show about Prince Charles." When no one said anything, she added: "It's on at eight."

"Thrown away the TVs?" Dad asked. Now he was looking annoyed.

"Yes!" Crystal wailed. "Every one of them!"

"Even the big-screen TV in the family room," I added softly.

Mom continued to frown at us all, a frown that seemed to hold a secret.

At that moment the front door opened again and Ashleigh stepped in. She's a round sort of person, with short, dark, feathery hair, and she's always wearing loose Indian-print dresses and interesting hats. Today she was wearing a red velvet hat with a silk flower on it. "Whoa!" she cried when she saw us in the hallway. "What's going on? Is it a council of war? I don't think I've seen you guys all in one place since Thanksgiving."

"We can talk later," Mom interrupted in a soft voice. But her tone was very firm. "I'm glad you're home early, Grant—and Ashleigh, too—our meal is ready."

"Meal?" Dad asked. "You mean dinner? And we're eating it all together?"

"Together," Mom affirmed pleasantly. Her frown had disappeared. "Come on now, let me take your coat and briefcase, and you just come with me. How about if I pour you a nice glass of wine to go with your meal? Now that Prohibition is officially over!" She giggled. "No need for bootlegging. You can drink your wine right out in the open. Here—just a little one. Now, the children must wash their hands. And Ashleigh, will you please light the candles?"

I didn't have a clue what Mom was talking about. I looked at Crystal. She was looking at Dad. Dad raised his eyebrows at Ashleigh. Ashleigh smiled at me and gave a tiny shrug. We all followed Mom down the hall in silence.

The table wasn't set in the kitchen. Instead, Mom led us to the formal dining room. I think I've eaten in that room only once or twice in living memory. The table was large and round, and now it was covered with a white cloth. Mom had set it with the silverware and plates and glasses that usually stay in the china closet. On a normal day we just grab forks from the drawers in the kitchen and eat in there. And we always, *always* watch the news or whatever while eating.

We all sat down. Crystal had her arms crossed like she meant to keep them that way. Dad was looking intrigued, as if this might be a surprise birthday party or something. Only Ashleigh had a little smile on her face, but she could afford to because it wasn't *her* mom who was being so strange.

I felt like we were out visiting people we didn't know very well. My knees bumped Mom's under the table. She turned to me and nodded. "Connor, will you please say grace?"

What was she on about now? "Grace," I said obediently.

"No, honey," replied Mom patiently. "It's a prayer. A prayer thanking God for our food."

I looked to Dad for help, but he was looking at Mom. So was Crystal. So was Ashleigh.

"Go on," prompted Mom.

"Okay." I remembered a movie I saw where there was a preacher or a rabbi or something standing up in front of a lot of people. "Dear Lord," I said in a loud voice that would reach to the very back of that kind of huge room. "Thank you for all this food. It smells really good." I glanced at Mom.

She smiled encouragingly. "Amen."

"Oh yeah. *Amen*," I added.

Crystal cleared her throat. "I'm getting really freaked out."

Mom started passing around platters of food that smelled, well, *heavenly*. Roast chicken with a tomato sauce, and mashed potatoes that I knew were the real thing, not the dried cubes or fake potato flakes that you mix with boiling water. I'd seen Mom with those potato peelings as proof. And there were green beans—real, fresh ones, not the frozen kind—cooked with lots of onions, and fluffy rolls and butter.

For a strange, shivery second I felt like I was in that painting in the art book. I looked at the door to the kitchen like maybe that grandma from the painting would waltz in with a big birthday cake. Then Crystal passed me the potatoes and broke the spell. Mom poured herself a glass of wine and held the glass up to the candlelight.

"Ah," she said. "Look at that sparkle." She took a sip. "Lovely, really delicious. That's what those Temperance folks forget—how perfectly delicious wine is. In moderation, of course. All things in moderation."

Crystal kicked me under the table. I kicked back because how was *I* supposed to know what Mom was talking about?

Dad raised his glass to Mom in a toast. "Kids, Mom is referring to the Temperance Movement," he told us. "In the late nineteenth century and early twentieth century, there was a push to do away with alcohol because it was thought to erode decent family values. The movement led to Prohibition—the Eighteenth Amendment to the Constitution—banning the sale and consumption of alcohol. It went into effect in 1920, I think I remember learning, and was repealed in 1933 or thereabouts."

Mom raised her glass to him. "Is that when they finally got rid of it? Such a silly law. One of the few bad things about the good old days."

"What good old days, Ms. Rigoletti?" asked Ashleigh.

Mom set down her glass. Her expression was composed, as if she'd been waiting for just such a question. "My dear ones," she began in her firm, lawyer voice, "we're going to turn right *now* into the good old days. I feel we've been missing out on a lot of things because we don't really see each other much, do we? I mean, we're a family, but we all keep to our own busy schedules..." Here she appealed to Dad. "Grant, you know how you and I haven't exactly been getting along lately? I'm sure it's because we haven't been spending enough time together."

Dad took a careful bite of chicken. "Listen, Pam," he said, chewing, "that might be true. But don't you think it's something we might discuss better alone? I mean"— and he cast his eye around the table at me and Crystal and Ashleigh—"like *in private*?"

"All right, dear," agreed Mom. "But I've been doing a lot of thinking over this past year or so—I mean, well, anyway, I know it might not be easy to change, but it's got to happen. For the sake of our family, some things are going to change around here."

"Like you've changed your clothes, Mom?" demanded Crystal. "And your hair?"

"First of all," continued Mom, ignoring the interruption, "I'm going to work only part-time. I'm going to cut back so that I can leave for work in the morning and be back home in Shady Grove by the time the first school bus comes by. So I'll be here, Crystal and Connor, when you get home from school."

"But—" began Crystal. "But I don't usually get home till nearly dinnertime, anyway."

That was true, but I didn't see why she was objecting. I kind of liked the idea that Mom would be around—especially if she would keep making cakes and stuff for after-school snacks.

"That's another thing," said Mom. "All these after-school classes have to stop. It's just too much—and it's not necessary. Now, children, I want you to think of all the classes and extracurricular clubs and sports you two are involved in, and pick *one or two* that are most important to you."

"What about the other ones?" I asked, seeing for a moment all my "extras" stacked up like building blocks in my mind. Soccer and karate and piano. Swimming and gymnastics and computer graphics. Baseball in the spring.

"The other ones we'll drop," said Mom simply. "You're both doing far too much."

My tower of blocks crashed onto the table. In my mind, I mean. But I could see them—all labeled SOCCER and KARATE and PIANO and everything. Which ones did I like best? Would I be sad without the others? I didn't really know.

"Don't we get any say in this?" demanded Crystal. "Don't we get to vote?"

"Women do have the right to vote now," Mom acknowledged, with a nod. "But you're not old enough yet. As your mother, I am making this decision for you."

"You're totally crazy!" cried Crystal.

Dad shushed her. "That's no way to talk to your mother." But he was darting apprehensive little looks over at Mom. He pinched the bridge of his nose and looked even more exhausted than he had earlier. "Is this about money, Pam?" he asked. "Are you worrying we can't afford these things? Because even if you cut back to part-time, we can certainly still pay for the kids' classes and extras."

"It's not about money," Mom said tightly. She took a bite of mashed potato. "It's about *family.*"

Ashleigh winked at me across the table.

She wasn't winking after she heard what Mom said next. Ashleigh's eyes popped like somebody's in a cartoon, and her mouth—full of nasty, chewed-up chicken—hung wide open.

"And we're going to cut back in other ways. The gardener's, Mrs. White's, even *your* services, Ashleigh, as our baby-sitter—these must go."

"But—what about my apartment here?" spluttered Ashleigh. "And the kids—who's going to get their meals and drive them places and everything?" I saw little flecks of chicken fly out onto the table. Good thing the cloth was white. She appealed to my dad. "Mr. Chase—what will I *do*?"

"You may still live in your apartment over the garage until you graduate," Mom assured her before Dad could say anything. "You know you're like one of the family. But we won't need you for Crystal and Connor anymore because *I* am going to be home with them. You can earn your keep by helping us out in other ways. You can help the children with the gardening, if you like, or the housecleaning. We can talk about specific duties and chores later."

"Earn my keep?" Ashleigh was frowning down at her plate now.

"Duties and chores?" squawked Crystal. *"Housecleaning?* You've got to be kidding!"

"Pam," said Dad in that tone I always think of as his heavy voice. "Pam, Pam. These are all big steps. Are you sure you've thought them through?"

"And what about the TVs?" I mumbled.

Crystal checked her watch.

"Grant, I'm as sure as I can be that these will be changes for the better. Toward a simpler, happier way of life. A happier family." Mom looked at Dad while she spoke, but I knew she meant what she said for all of us at the table. She folded her napkin (a *cloth* napkin?) and laid it next to her plate. "Things have to change. And we're going to go cold turkey."

"Turkey?" I blurted out, totally confused, because we were eating *chicken*. Even though they're sort of the same thing.

"Cold turkey," repeated Mom. "That means just quitting. Just stopping—just like that." She snapped her fingers. "Like Mrs. White quit smoking. One day she smoked, then one day she'd stopped. No gradual cutting back, no weaning herself away from her addictive habit—just cold-turkey quitting."

"Like, you think we're drug addicts?" snapped Crystal. I just sat back and listened, letting her fight this particular battle. Not because I didn't mind losing the TVs—I did. But because I had this gut feeling we were going to lose the battle. Lose the whole war, in fact.

"TV is addictive," Mom replied calmly. "Things are going to change around here. The Rigoletti-Chase family is turning over a new leaf."

When she said that, I pictured the big book, its pages turning slowly.

"But *why*?" Crystal demanded urgently. "What's wrong with the way we are already?"

Mom laughed, but it wasn't a cheerful sound.

"We're *fine*, Pam," said Dad impatiently now. He pushed back his chair, leaving his salad uneaten, and stood up. "If you want to talk about getting into family counseling or something, I suppose we could. I mean, I sure don't see the need, but if it's what you want—"

Mom sighed. "Every Thanksgiving," she said softly, "we eat our feast in a restaurant."

I stared at her. What did that have to do with anything? My teacher, Ms. Rose, would have said that was a non sequitur. That's what she always tells kids when they just blurt out something that doesn't have anything to do with anything.

"Yes," said Dad, nodding cautiously. "We all agree Hannigans is the nicest place to eat." He sat down again.

Mom twisted her wedding ring on her finger. "There we are at a lovely, expensive restaurant, eating food some chef has prepared for the crowds, surrounded by people we don't know. I used to think it was just fine—a fine way to celebrate. But I've had time to think, and I want some changes around here. We never eat together as a family at home—never! Not even on Thanksgiving. We have this dining room and never use it. We're never home at the same time, Grant, except to sleep. I hardly even remember how to cook, and I hardly see my kids because other people are taking care of them..." She looked down at her hands and twisted her ring a few more times. The diamonds sparkled in the candlelight.

Slowly she reached for her wineglass and lifted it. She held it out slightly, as if to make a toast, and she smiled, as if she were about to speak. We waited. And waited. We were all silent, staring at her. The whole house seemed so quiet. No TV babbling in the background. Just us, just breathing. All of us just like the family in the painting, frozen for all time.

I could hear the clock ticking in the hallway. Mom still sat there, glass held aloft, smile fixed, not moving. But then I saw her terror-filled eyes—and I realized that she *couldn't* move.

A shiver pounced down my spine.

"Pam?" Dad said softly. "Pam?"

"Ms. Rigoletti?" whispered Ashleigh.

"Do something, somebody!" Crystal yelled, but she was staring at me.

I stood up and took the wineglass out of Mom's rigid fingers. I held her hand in mine and squeezed it. It felt cold, like the hand of a hard plastic doll. Sucking in my breath to hold in my own growing terror, I reached out and put my arms around her in an awkward hug. "Mom?" I said. Then louder, right in her ear: *"Mom!"*

She jumped as if waking from a bad dream and let out a little shriek. "Goodness, Connor! Lower your voice. There's no need to use such a strident voice in the house. Save that for the playground, if you please."

"But, Mom—" I began.

"Pam, what happened to you?" My dad came to her side as I stepped away. "I think you were having some sort of seizure!"

She turned her face to his. "Oh, Grant. I don't think so . . ." But her voice was trembling. There was a long silence. Then Mom shrugged. "It seems to have passed, anyway. I'm fine now."

"So, can I watch my show about Prince Charles,

Mom? It starts in just a few minutes. Maybe we can all watch it together. You know, the whole family together, really cozy and everything?" Trust Crystal to be the one to bring things back to normal.

Mom shook her head. "No, Crystal," she said. "We're going cold turkey. That's the way I broke my own habit—and it's the best way—"

"Wait a sec—*when* did you break your habit?" I interrupted. "I heard your TV on in your bedroom just last night!" I turned to Dad. "Wasn't she watching TV last night? Or the night before?"

Dad cleared his throat a few times before answering, but when he did speak, he was on another track. "You didn't really throw the TVs away, did you, Pam? Not, like, out in the *trash,* right? That would be going a little bit far, I think. Those sets cost *bucks.*"

"Let's just say they've been safely removed from the scene," Mom replied serenely. Her voice was back to normal now. Dad looked hugely relieved.

"Now," continued Mom, "dinnertime is conversation time. Let's hear about how your day went. Crys, you may go first."

"Go where?" growled Crystal in her nastiest tone.

"Tell us about your day, dear. The high and low points."

Crystal just glowered at her. "This is definitely the low point," she muttered.

I just kept eating. So did Ashleigh and Dad. We all felt there'd been enough talking already at this meal.

But the meal *was* delicious, we had to admit. "And

isn't it amazing," Dad said when we'd finished, "that we've actually sat here for nearly an hour all together—and the phone hasn't rung even once?"

Mom smiled a secret smile. "That's because I turned off all the phones. *And* the pagers. No ringing and beeping disturbing meals anymore. Not in *our* home."

*T*hat night after dinner Mom made us help her clean the dishes and wipe the counters. Then she tried to shepherd us all into the family room, but Crystal was so pissed about missing Prince Charles that she stomped upstairs to her room and wouldn't come down, even when Dad bellowed for her. And Ashleigh escaped to her apartment over the garage with the excuse that she had to study. I'd bet anything she was watching one of her shows, but if she was, she kept the sound down so nobody heard it.

I sat there on the family-room couch between Dad and Mom. Mom asked Dad to read aloud from *The Wind in the Willows*, even though we already saw the video. I sat there trying to listen to the book. On video it's a cool story about these animals called Toad and Mole and Badger who have all these adventures on the riverbank. In the film Toad is really hysterical, totally proud and boastful. He lives in Toad Hall, his mansion, and he drives like a maniac. I kept waiting for Dad to get to that part, but listening to a book isn't like watching TV. There aren't any pictures to keep you interested, so you have to imagine everything for yourself. I kept thinking about other things, like how I was going to tell

Doug all about Mom tomorrow and how Crystal and I still hadn't shown Dad the paintings by Fitzgerald Cotton. I glanced over at Mom to see if she was listening to the story. She had her eyes closed and her head tipped back against the couch pillows. She might have been totally into the story, or she might have been sound asleep, for all I could tell. Or she might have fallen into another trance.

"Mom!" I shouted, jostling her arm.

"Good heavens, Connor, what has gotten into you tonight?" she cried, her eyes flying open. "Can't you just sit still and listen to a few chapters?" She shook her head, turning to my dad. "See, Grant? Too much TV. Destroys kids' imaginations so they have no attention span."

"Sorry," I said. "Sorry, Mom." I settled back on the couch. "Go on, Dad. I'm listening already!"

And I did try to listen. I tried very hard to concentrate, but my mind was ticking along at a zillion miles a minute trying to make sense of what was going on in our house. When Dad finally finished reading, I said I was going upstairs to bed. And Mom said she'd be up in a few minutes to tuck me in and kiss me good night. And would I like a bedtime story?

Bedtime tucking and kissing were things she hadn't done since I was, like, *two.* "Sure, Mom. Whatever."

I really did head for the stairs. But then I detoured into the living room. I wanted to get that book of paintings and look at it again, and I wanted to show it to Dad.

I looked everywhere. On the coffee table. The bookshelves. The couch. *Under* the couch. But the book was gone—as if it had never been there at all.

Then I saw Mom watching me from the doorway, and her eyes weren't full of terror—they were full of something else. A hardness—a coldness—that made her seem like she was a different person altogether standing there watching me. I didn't bother to ask her about the book. Somehow I knew what she'd say.

I just scurried past her up the stairs and dived into my bed. She didn't come up to kiss me, after all. And there was no bedtime story, either.

∽ Chapter 4 ∽

The Key Chain

"Remember that movie we saw where the kid's mom turns out to be an alien?" I asked Doug as we sat in the school cafeteria the next day. "I think that's what's happened at my house, for real." He just sort of gaped at me. "They got my real mom, and left one of *them* in her place, all disguised."

"Sure, Connor. Whatever you say." But he looked interested.

Usually *Doug's* the one with stuff to tell. His mom is in the news a lot because she keeps getting elected for all sorts of things in state politics, and she moved to Washington, D.C., last spring to work with the president on some special commission. No one knows for sure when she'll be home again. Doug and his sister get to visit her during school vacations, though. And Doug's dad is a famous rock climber who is hardly ever home because he's breaking records scaling the highest mountains all around the world. Doug is afraid he'll break his neck, but so far that hasn't happened; if you ask me, it'll be Doug's little sister, Becca, who breaks her neck first. Becca is only five, and she's always doing stuff to drive Doug crazy. One Saturday morning just last month, she managed to climb up on top of their refrigerator and leap over to the top pantry shelf, where she hung by the tips of her fingers—screaming her head off—until Doug finally heard her. Their nanny was still asleep and wouldn't have heard a stampede of rhinoceroses—she's that old. Anyway, Becca was just trying to be a mountain climber, like Mr. Ito, but Doug told her she could have been killed. For a whole week after that, he let Becca carry his *Star Wars* key chain around for good luck and safe landings. It has a red light that flashes when your palm warms the metal Death Star, and Doug says it might have magical powers, like a charm. He says he always aces his tests when he has it in his pocket.

Doug tells me all sorts of interesting stories every day, and usually all I have to say is stuff about what I watched on TV or how sickening Ashleigh sounds talking to her boyfriend on the phone while Crystal and I are eating dinner. But now, finally, like it or not, I had some real news.

"What's so weird about her?" Doug asked me now.

"She's thrown out all our TVs," I reported. "*And* disconnected my computer and PlayStation and taken my phone. Crystal's, too. And she's going to work part-time. *And*"—I'd saved the weirdest for last—"she cooked dinner last night. From *scratch*."

Doug jingled his *Star Wars* key chain. "Freaky."

"Yeah." But I wasn't sure how to tell him about the

art book or the way Mom kept freezing up. I wanted to check that book again to see if maybe I'd only imagined how much the woman in those paintings looked like Mom.

"Hey, you want to come over after karate?" Doug asked. "You could stay for dinner, too. We're ordering pizza."

"Yeah." I felt relief course through me at the thought of going home with Doug rather than back to my own house—where who *knew* what Mom would be doing?

But it turned out not to be so easy. Doug and I both had karate after school, then rode the last bus home. As we were walking up the street to Doug's house, I heard a voice calling to us.

"Yoo-hoo, Connor!"

Yoo-hoo? I glanced across the street, and there was Mom in our front yard, raking leaves.

"Mom!" I stopped so abruptly on the sidewalk that Doug crashed right into me. I didn't know she'd *already* cut back on her job.

"There you are!" she cried, her voice sounding really happy. "The very boys I've been waiting for."

She was wearing jeans and a big sweatshirt, just as if it were a Saturday instead of a weekday. And she had been working hard, I could see that, pulling into a big pile by our fence all the leaves that had fallen from the ash tree. Her cheeks were bright red from the wind, and she looked way younger than a mom should look.

"Come on, boys! I've got a lovely leaf pile for you to

jump in, and when you're finished playing, there are oatmeal cookies cooling in the kitchen."

Leaf pile? I was embarrassed. "I was going to Doug's," I mumbled.

My mom dropped her rake in the pile of dry leaves and walked over to us. "No, I want you home. But you're welcome to come in and share Connor's snack, Doug."

"Cool," he said to Mom.

"You two finish up here, and I'll go make you some hot cocoa to go with the cookies," Mom said, and she handed me the rake.

She turned and went into the house, closing the door. I hardly dared to look at Doug. But when I did, he was just standing there, staring after Mom.

"Wow," he said. "Cookies and cocoa?"

I shrugged. "I told you, *aliens.*"

"Yeah, I can see that." Doug shook his head. "I thought you were kidding." He kicked at some leaves. "Well, let's do these fast. What happened to your gardener?"

"Mom said we don't need him anymore." I started raking, and Doug stuffed the leaves into the big green bin. Neither one of us actually jumped in the big pile of leaves. But when all the leaves were cleared away, I sort of wished we had. It might have been fun.

We went in and had our snack, and Crystal came home and had a cookie, too. Mom asked Doug if he'd like to stay for dinner, and he said sure. He phoned his nanny, then Mom sent us up to my room to *play,* but she made Crystal stay down in the kitchen to cut up vegetables for the stew. We could hear Crystal's complaining, even with my bedroom door closed.

It seemed really *weird* just to be sitting there without any computer games or anything. Like, what were we supposed to *do*? Doug was looking totally bored, and I'm pretty sure it was only the smell of the beef stew that kept him from running home to his pizza next door.

"I didn't know your mom could cook," said Doug, with a sidelong glance over at me. "Or is Mrs. White here today?"

"Nope. Somehow Mom's learned to cook—*and* she told Mrs. White we don't need her anymore," I replied. "Just like she told the gardener. *And* Ashleigh."

"Seriously freaky," Doug said.

"Tell me about it." I scuffed my shoes on the carpet. There wasn't a single thing in the whole world to do. Doug just sat next to me, jingling his *Star Wars* key chain, looking around as if maybe something would happen. But nothing did.

"So, did you see *Mad Scientist* last night?" he asked after a while. "It was the one about the gun dealers arming the corpses, and then the scientist brought them back to life—it was so gruesome!"

"Oh, yeah, I've seen that one before," I replied. *Mad Scientist* was one of my favorite shows, and I'd seen all the episodes. Now they were showing only reruns. Not that I'd be able to watch even reruns anymore.

We sat in silence again, and I could even hear the ticking of the hallway clock. I could also hear Crystal whining down in the kitchen. Doug shifted on the bed, and I bet he was thinking about leaving, and I almost wanted him to leave because it was so embarrassing just sitting there.

But then I had an idea of something we could do. Something I should have done already but didn't quite have the guts to do all alone.

"Want to see something?" I asked Doug.

"Sure." But he didn't even look at me.

"Come on, then," I said, standing up. "But be quiet. We can't let my mom hear us or she'll go ballistic."

Now Doug looked at me with a spark of interest. "Hear what?"

I led him silently down the stairs to the living room. "There's a book you have to see," I whispered to Doug. But the big art book wasn't back on the coffee table. I scanned the shelves. It wasn't there, either.

"What?" hissed Doug.

"Shhh," I said. "She's hidden it someplace. Come on, let's look." I peeked into the kitchen. No book, and no Mom, but Crystal was there, chopping potatoes with quick, angry thrusts. When she saw me and Doug, she raised her knife threateningly. We ducked out again and looked into the family room.

Mom was there, knitting something out of soft green yarn.

Knitting? I didn't think Mom even knew how to knit. In fact, I *knew* she didn't know how, because she always laughed about ladies who did knit, and said she couldn't see spending time twisting yarn around little sticks when you could buy perfectly elegant sweaters ready-made from Nordstrom or Bloomingdale's or from any of the fine catalogs.

And now, here was Mom, knitting. No, wait—she *had* been knitting, but now she was just *sitting* there with the yarn on her lap, her hands holding the needles in position like crossed swords. She wasn't moving a muscle.

I felt a flutter of fear in my stomach—that moth batting against a lightbulb. *"Mom,"* I whispered.

"What's she doing?" hissed Doug. He stared wide-eyed at my mom. We walked over to stand in front of her. "Look at that smile..."

She was smiling the same teasing smile I'd seen in the art book, with the same lift to the chin and quirk to the eyebrows, as if she were playfully daring someone to snap her photo. Someone unseen—

But in her eyes was a look of terror. Worse than terror this time. Her neck muscles were taut, bulging—as if she were struggling to move her head but couldn't. Her nostrils were flared.

"Mom!" I grabbed her arm—and she suddenly relaxed.

"Oh, Connor—thank you. I was—stuck."

"Stuck?" I asked wildly. "What do you mean, *stuck*?"

Mom just looked at me as if she had no idea what she'd meant.

Then Crystal shouted a bad word in the kitchen and Mom jumped up, dropping the green wool. "No cursing in this house, young lady, or you'll be grounded for a month!" Mom called. "I'm ashamed of you."

"Well, you should be ashamed of yourself," Crystal retorted, appearing in the doorway, "making me into your *servant* just so you can save money and not hire Mrs. White anymore!"

I stood there, still holding Mom's arm. The skin felt cold—with the muscles underneath tight and hard—as if Mom really had been frozen and was just starting to thaw again.

"Now you're being silly," Mom told Crystal mildly. "Every girl needs to learn to cook."

"No way!"

"*And* to mind her manners."

I jerked my head at Doug, and he followed me out of the room. We were just tiptoeing across the hallway to the living room, when I stopped, aghast at what Mom was saying next.

"And it's not only girls who need to know how to keep house these days." Mom's voice was still cheerful. "Women didn't get the vote just to stay home and clean house. They're going out into the world—and into the workforce. Men are going to have to get used to sharing their offices. *And* they'll have to learn to help out more at home, cleaning and cooking and caring for the children."

Then there was a pause for a second like she was thinking things over. I hoped she was going to take back the part about cooking, but instead she laughed gaily and said, "Silly me—of course women have been out working for *years!*"

"Like about a hundred," Crystal snorted, but I bet she felt as scared as I did about Mom's talk of working women and voting. "Anyway, who would want to eat anything *Connor* cooked?"

I agreed with Crystal. No way.

In the living room I scanned the shelves again but saw no sign of the big art book. So I grabbed Doug's arm and propelled him out of the room and back up the stairs before my mom saw us.

Doug and I hurried down the hallway to my parents' big master suite. It had a sitting room decorated in whites and golds, with royal blue velvet furniture. The master bedroom had a king-sized bed covered in a white-and-gold duvet, topped with gold-tassled royal blue velvet pillows. Both rooms looked perfect—clean and elegant, with not one stray sock out of place. They looked as frozen as my mom had. *Just as—as posed,* I thought. And quite suddenly, I wanted to jump on the bed and rumple all those pillows. But I carefully checked out the stack of books on the bedside table without touching a thing. None of the books was *the* book.

There were two bathrooms—his and hers—also done in blue and gold and white. In Dad's I found copies of *Money* magazine in a wicker basket. That was it. Nothing at all to read in Mom's—or so I thought. As I was turning to leave the room, my eye caught sight of something peeking out from the half-open door of the linen closet. Something brown and green that didn't match the blue and white and gold towels.

I opened the linen-closet door. *Yes!*

I reached in carefully, holding my breath as if I were approaching a rare and possibly dangerous animal. I slid the art book out from under the towels and held it out to Doug in triumph.

"Cotton in the Twentieth Century?" Doug read aloud in a hiss, disappointment coloring his voice. I knew he'd probably been expecting a book about magical spells—like the ones on *Mad Scientist* about how to raise the dead and teach them to shoot. Something like that.

"Don't worry," I told him, hugging the book. "You want to see this. You really do."

Doug didn't look convinced, but I knew he would see what I meant as soon as I showed him the paintings. I led the way out of the bathroom, through the bedroom, back into the sitting room—heading back for my own bedroom—when we heard footsteps coming up the stairs. We froze.

"Someone's coming," Doug whispered. He had a big grin on his face now; suddenly he was having fun. But my heart was thumping hard, and I pulled him back into the master bedroom. It was either my mom or Crystal coming. If it was Crystal, those footsteps would stop at the top of the stairs, where her bedroom was.

But the footsteps kept coming along the hallway, tapping on the shiny hardwood floor.

I wrenched the handle on the massive mirrored closet and, pulling the door open, shoved Doug inside and followed right after him. I pulled the door closed just as I heard Mom come into the bedroom.

The closet was dark, but I could sense Doug was standing next to me, trying not to giggle. He kept flicking the red light on his *Star Wars* key chain on and off, on and off. Was he using his good-luck charm to ward off trouble—or was this just a game to him? *I* knew it was no game. There was something serious going on, something real, and the book was part of it. I sucked in my breath silently when I heard the bedsprings creak as Mom sat down. We waited, then I heard the bed creak again as Mom stood up and walked—where?

I peeked out and saw her heading for the bathroom. If I was lucky, she just had to pee.

But then I heard the linen-closet door slam, and she came back into the bedroom, then out into the hallway. "Connor! Crystal? *Where is my book?*" Her voice was angry, yes, and outraged. But there was a note of something else in it, too.

A note of absolute hysteria.

"*Whoa!*" Doug burst out, his breath coming hot on the side of my face. "You'd better give her book back!"

"No, not yet." I edged the door open, my heart hammering hard. Mom had run downstairs, so I darted down the hall, into my bedroom, and quickly slid the book behind my dresser. Then I flopped down onto my desk chair. Doug collapsed onto the bed, and both of us contrived to look as though we'd been there all the time, bored out of our minds.

"What?" I asked when Mom ran back up the stairs and appeared in my doorway, hands on her hips, eyes blazing.

"My book!" she cried. "Where is it?"

"Which one?" I asked innocently.

"You know the book. The one you were looking at last night."

I shook my head. "Isn't it on the coffee table?"

"No." She hugged herself suddenly, looking lost. "Crystal swears she didn't take it. Did you, Connor? Because it isn't yours to take! It's a very important, very valuable old book."

I just kept shaking my head.

"Well, if you see it, Connor, I need it back. I need it—" Mom turned away as her voice cracked. She took a shuddering breath. "If you see it, please bring it to me immediately. And do not open it. Do you understand? There is a *valuable* old paper inside. You must not touch it!" She hesitated. "It could be..."

The unspoken word hung in the air: *dangerous.*

"Okay, Mom," I said in the same gentle voice I once used on a wild-looking dog who menaced me in the grocery store parking lot. *Down girl. Atta girl.*

"Is dinner almost ready?" Doug asked. "Because I have to be home by seven."

That was the right thing to say. Mom took a deep breath. "Yes," she said. "Dinner is ready, and you boys should come downstairs right now." She ran her hand over her hair, smoothing the new, short curls.

I heard the grind of the garage door opening. "Dad's home early again," I said. "Maybe *he* took your book."

We all went downstairs, Mom still pale and trembling, Doug looking excited, and me with my stomach throbbing in fear—and relief—and probably even hunger.

The stew really did smell delicious.

We ate in the dining room, as we had the night before. This time Mom didn't ask anyone else, but just said a simple prayer herself. Ashleigh complimented Crystal on the stew. Crystal grumbled about how she nearly cut off her thumb, chopping carrots. And Dad urged more helpings of potatoes and bread and salad on everyone. "I could get used to feasting like this every night," he said approvingly, but a little worried frown creased his forehead.

Doug ate and ate. He ate like he could hardly believe how good it was. He cooperated politely with Mom, telling us all about the high and low points of his day.

But I was too worried about the book hidden in my bedroom to enjoy the food or conversation. The stew might have been cold pizza as far as I was concerned.

I felt a strange prickling at the back of my neck, and I imagined I could sense the big art book waiting for me, almost calling to me to come. I imagined it inching its way out from behind my dresser, thumping onto the floor, the pages fluttering in a breeze until they stopped turning right at the very page where *Elsie's Party* was in full swing. I actually had to jump up from the table and run out of the room without even excusing myself—just to check.

The book was still there behind my dresser.

I heard Mom calling me from the foot of the stairs. "Sorry," I said, walking back downstairs. "I had to—um—go to the bathroom."

She frowned at me. "Manners, Connor."

Right after dessert—homemade apple pie with ice cream—Doug had to go home. He lingered in the hallway while my mom wrapped up a piece of pie for him to take home to Becca.

"You never showed me the book!" he hissed at me.

"Next time," I whispered.

"After school tomorrow, okay? After soccer practice."

"Okay," I agreed as my mom came back into the front hall and handed Doug the foil-wrapped pie. But I knew there was no way I could wait that long. The art book was practically screaming to me now—it was a wonder the whole neighborhood didn't hear it calling me:

Come to me . . . come back! I'll die without you!

Chapter 5

Hidden Pictures

I felt shaky and sort of sick, but first I helped Dad clean the dishes. Crystal did her homework at the kitchen table. We could hear Mom upstairs opening closets and slamming drawers, and my stomach clenched with each thump. Mom was looking for her book. Dad kept glancing over his shoulder, and I thought maybe Mom's banging around up there was getting to him.

"Don't bother, Dad," Crystal said sourly. "You can look around all you like, but no TV is going to appear. I've checked everywhere. There is not a single TV anywhere in this house."

Dad looked sheepish. "Well, maybe Mom was right to store them away for a while," he said slowly. "Because I'm having withdrawal symptoms—and you don't have those unless you're addicted to something."

I rubbed the stew pot dry with a clean dish towel. "I bet she took them all to the dump."

Dad shook his head. "She promised me that she

didn't throw them out." He reached for the newspaper, delivered that morning, still lying unopened on the counter. Dad pulled off the rubber band and unrolled the paper. "She's acting oddly—I'll give you that, kids. But I think we ought to go along with her for a while." He leafed through the paper. "We can just read, I guess." I wiped the countertop while he turned a few more pages. Then he dropped the paper onto the counter. "Or— maybe I'll go visit Ashleigh for a little while."

"I'm coming with you!" Crystal leaped up from her chair.

"Finish your homework," Dad said. "You don't even like to watch hockey."

"Neither does Ashleigh," Crystal retorted. "And at least it will be *something* to watch."

They were just leaving the kitchen when we all heard Mom's footsteps running down the stairs. "Connor!" she yelled.

I turned the water on full force in the sink to rinse my sponge. "In the kitchen!" I called over the din.

Mom appeared in the doorway. Her face was red and her voice was trembling. "Connor! What is the meaning of *this*?"

This was Doug's *Star Wars* key chain. Its little red light flashed in Mom's hand. My stomach clenched again; it felt like someone had punched me.

"That's Doug's," I said, surprised that my voice came out sounding halfway normal.

"Indeed it is," she said. "And what was it doing on the floor of my closet, may I ask?"

"Your closet?" I squeaked. "What would Doug be doing in your closet?" I screwed up my face like I was trying to think.

"Doug's a little sneak," Crystal announced from the doorway. "I found him in my room once, snooping in my desk. He said he was looking for the *Mad Scientist* software. Right! Like anyone's going to believe *that*!"

"Well, maybe that's what he was doing in your closet," I said hurriedly. "I mean, with my computer gone, and PlayStation and everything, we didn't have anything to do. I told him I didn't know where you'd stashed everything. Maybe when he went down the hall to use the bathroom, he just thought he'd check the closets or something. Maybe he wasn't really *snooping*—maybe just trying to help me out..."

Dad put his arm around Mom's tense shoulders. "Pam," he said in his sweetest voice. "Speaking of helping out, my love, where *have* you stashed them? There's a hockey game I'm dying to see—"

Mom handed me the key chain with a sigh. She turned to Dad and rubbed her fingers over her eyes. She looked tired, seemed defeated. She sank onto one of the stools at the counter.

And then it happened again. Worse than ever this time.

She jerked, then stiffened. Her lips curled back from her teeth in a terrible smile. Her eyes were wide with panic. She was frozen stiff—but a deep groan spilled up out of her, the sound of someone trying to wake from a nightmare.

"Pam!" cried Dad, and he wrapped his arms around her. Each time she'd frozen like this before, touch had brought her out of it, but this time nothing happened. Dad held her and sort of shook her, but she sat like a stone on that stool, except that stones never make noises like someone being tortured. There were no drops of blood though, this time.

"*Aahhhhgghh!*" she cried. "*Aaaghh ... aaaghh ...*" And then, "No! Noooo!"

Dad dropped his head to her chest and listened to her heartbeat. He grabbed her hand and tried to turn it so he could feel the pulse in the wrist, but it was like trying to turn steel. "Kids," he cried to us. "Her pulse is weak. Her heart rate seems too slow—"

"Mom!" screamed Crystal. "Mom, what's happening to you?" She grabbed my arm. "Quick, Con, call nine-one-one!" But as I whirled over to the phone, grateful that Mom had at least left us a couple modern conveniences, her voice stopped me.

"Wait!" she gasped. She closed her mouth and her eyes blinked a few times, rapidly, as if she had some specks of dirt in them. "Oh my!"

"Pam, are you all right? What happened, darling?" Dad bent over her, worried, still with his arms around her.

She reached up and patted his hand. "I just—just felt dizzy for a second. That's all."

Crystal and I stared at each other. Dad stroked Mom's hair. "You're scaring us, Pam. I really think you had a seizure. We'd better call the doctor."

"Now, don't be silly!" Mom laughed and unwrapped

Dad's arms. "I'm perfectly fine." Then she caught sight of the newspaper on the counter and snatched it up, all the stiffness suddenly gone. She tapped a picture on the front page. "Is that one still president?" she asked with a laugh. "Seems like somebody else would have been elected by now." She flipped through the pages. "Whoa—look at the real estate prices..." She stood there reading the paper like current events were so fascinating. Like she'd been gone on a long trip to some remote spot and now had a lot of catching up to do.

"Pam, let me call Dr. Rhodes." Dad stroked her hand, then lifted her wrist, tracking the pulse.

"Why bother her? I'm *fine*," Mom said, pulling her hand away. She rustled the paper. "Look here, Grant. Can you believe these prices?"

Dad cleared his throat. "It's *you* I can't believe, Pam."

But it looked like Mom was all right again. Not *normal,* but not frozen, either. I waited around for a few seconds, trying to figure out if she really didn't remember what had just happened to her—or if she was just trying to keep us from worrying. Then I decided this was as good a chance as any to escape, so I sidled quietly out of the kitchen. I did not miss the look Crystal gave me as I passed her, and so I was not surprised when I heard her right behind me on the stairs.

"I think it *is* a brain tumor," she said. "It's got to be. I've heard they can cause seizures and things." She sounded like she was about to cry.

"Somehow I don't think it is," I said slowly. "No, I think it's something else."

"Like what?" she demanded.

"I don't know. But I'm going to find out." I was at the top of the stairs. "I'm *trying* to find out."

"Is that what you and Doug were doing in Mom's closet?" she hissed.

"Come to my room," I whispered. "I'll show you."

I closed my bedroom door behind us and clicked the lock. Then I went over to the dresser. I pulled out the big art book and carried it to the bed. Crystal and I sat cross-legged on the bed and paged through the book. "I was going to show Doug," I told her. "But Mom had hidden it..." And I related how we'd searched for the book and found it, and how Mom had come upstairs just at that moment and we'd had to run for cover.

"Stupid Doug and his stupid key chain!" Crystal said.

"Yeah, well, it doesn't really matter." I tapped the page with my finger. "This is what matters." But what I just couldn't figure out was *why* it mattered. Or how Mom could be so different just since yesterday.

We stared down at *Elsie's Party, 1926*.

"That isn't Mom," Crystal said slowly. "It just can't be. It's impossible."

I rubbed my finger on the picture of the woman at the table who looked like Mom—or her clone. "Same hair," I said.

"Mom *obviously* just copied the hairstyle in this book," said Crystal witheringly.

"But look at the earrings," I whispered, and I felt my heart thumping hard in my chest. You could see it perfectly clearly when you looked closely: There were tiny dangly pendants painted on the woman's ears, peeking out from beneath her curls. Little gold elephants. "They look like the ones Dad had specially made for her birthday last year."

Crystal wrapped her long ponytail around and around her hand, something she always does when she is nervous or upset. "It's just a coincidence!" she hissed at me. "It has to be. What possible connection could Mom have to some woman who looked just like her and had the same earrings around eighty years ago?" She shook her head and answered her own question before I could say anything. "No connection at all, that's what! In fact, this might not even have been a real person! The artist could have just made up somebody out of his head. Artists do that all the time."

"But, Crys," I said in a low voice, trying to puzzle it out in my own mind, "how can you explain all these pictures?" I flipped through the book. "Look, this one on the couch, holding a rose—I found Mom just like *that* when I came home. And this one, chopping onions? She was doing the exact same thing—and sort of standing there, frozen, as if she were—"

Crystal jumped off my bed. "I agree that Mom is being totally weird," she said briskly, "but it can't be anything to do with this book, and I think you'd better just put it back where you found it." She slammed the door and stomped down the stairs.

I sat there on my bed and kept turning the pages in the big book. Fitzgerald Cotton's paintings were divided into three categories. The first section was titled "Early

Work," the second was called "The Muse Period," and the third was called "The Dark Years." I turned to "Early Work" first, mostly boring landscapes with old falling-down barns and fences, painted in sort of dull grays and browns and dark reds, with no people in the pictures at all.

The muse-period paintings were bright and vibrant. These were the ones that all, incredibly, featured my mom. There was Mom knitting, weeding a garden, wearing a white dress and hat, leaning over a bed of daffodils. Mom laughing under a canopy of giant sunflowers. Mom playing checkers with a little boy in an old-fashioned kitchen. Mom curled up on a couch, with a fire in the fireplace, reading a book to four kids—two boys and two girls—who sat at her feet, toasting marshmallows on long sticks. Mom and the grandmotherly woman from *Elsie's Party*, sitting on a front porch, drinking lemonade.

I turned the pages silently, chewing the inside of my cheek. Chewing hard. The paintings of the muse period were so clear and detailed, they looked almost like photos. Until you saw the brush strokes, I mean.

"It has to be Mom; it *has* to be," I whispered, and I traced my finger over a portrait of *Muse in Straw Hat, 1926,* the gold elephant earrings just visible. I read swiftly from the book:

> *Fitzgerald Cotton's health, always fragile, took a turn for the worse after the death of his beloved younger brother, Homer, in the final days of World War I. He and Homer had been very close as boys,*

with the more robust Homer looking after his frail, artistic brother, Fitzgerald. After Homer Cotton's death, Fitzgerald Cotton's creative genius was stilled. For years he could not paint, and he became more and more depressed. His behavior grew erratic and increasingly strange, and his parents feared for his sanity. They urged him to move back to his childhood home in Shady Grove, California, to let them care for him. They arranged for him to travel in Europe in 1924, after he told them that his lifelong dream was to study Renaissance painting in Italy, the land of his ancestors.

While studying in Padua, Cotton traced his own roots through a direct bloodline back to Lorenzo da Padova, a fifteenth-century painter of the Magi School. Cotton returned to California in 1925, his artistic drive restored. His work took on new intensity, with hints of da Padova's brilliant style.

The appearance some months later, in the spring of 1925, of the mysterious woman Cotton referred to as his muse is credited by many art critics and scholars as instrumental in breaking through Cotton's depression, though other scholars maintain that it was Cotton's use of rare, ancient paints obtained during his Italian sojourn—paints reputedly once belonging to Lorenzo da Padova himself—that gave his art new life. Nonetheless, Cotton's painter's block was ended. The body of work painted between 1925 and 1926 features his anonymous muse and is imbued with a fresh style and vibrancy.

I stopped reading. "I don't believe it," I said flatly, right out loud as if Doug or Crystal or somebody were there to argue with me. "Mom wasn't even *born* in 1926. Even her *parents* weren't born yet! It just doesn't make sense."

I wished Doug or Crystal were there. I didn't like being alone with this. Whatever *this* was. My eyes scanned the next page.

After a year, Cotton's muse disappeared as suddenly as she'd appeared. Cotton's painting style changed again. His work became dark and sinister. The cheerful vibrancy of the muse period was gone forever, replaced by the undertone of menace that haunted Cotton's work until his death by suicide, in 1928.

I turned the pages, staring down at grim, grainy-looking paintings, all grays and blacks and blues, with strange swirling shapes that reminded me of ships lost at sea. In some of the paintings there was a little face of a man down in the right-hand corner, with a creepy, unpleasant smile. I wondered if that was what Fitzgerald Cotton had looked like. I wasn't sure what "undertone of menace" meant, but I sure didn't like Cotton's later work.

Then the door to my bedroom crashed open, hitting the wall, and Mom stood there, cheeks red and eyes blazing. I edged toward the wall, suddenly understanding "undertone of menace" perfectly. If Mom hadn't already taken my phone away, I might have grabbed it and dialled 9-1-1.

Mom approached the bed. She slapped her hand down hard on the book like she wished it were *me* she was hitting. Her voice came out tight and controlled and icy. I'd never seen her so mad in my whole life—not even when I spilled my Coke all over my computer once and wrecked the whole thing. But there was something else, too, besides mad.

"I told you this is *my* book. I told you not to touch it." Her voice squeaked a little at the end, and I saw that behind her icy anger, she was so scared she was shaking. Her fear made me remember this was my *mom,* not some crazy witch, no matter how weird she was acting.

So I took a deep breath, like Ashleigh always tells me to when Crystal's bugging me. "Mom," I said quietly. "Tell me about the pictures."

"You saw them?" asked Mom, her voice squeaking again in what sounded to me like panic. *"All of them?"* She bent over the book and flicked frantically through the pages. Then she picked up the heavy book and shook it. A piece of folded paper fluttered out of the back and she caught it in a quick swoop. "Not all of them!" she cried. "Not *this* one!"

"Let me see it," I said.

"You can't," said Mom, folding the paper and putting it behind her back. "You mustn't see this. You'd never understand." But something in her eyes looked to me like she might be wavering, like maybe she really *did* want to show somebody.

"How could Fitzgerald Cotton paint you before you were even born, Mom?" I whispered. "How could he paint these"—I reached out a trembly finger and touched the gold elephants that dangled from her ears—"before Dad ever gave them to you?"

Mom was watching me closely. There were tears in her eyes.

I felt I was just on the brink of understanding something, something so weird that it couldn't be grasped. It was too impossible.

"Tell me what happened to you, Mom," I said urgently. "Tell me what's *still* happening—"

But it was too late. Even as I spoke to her, it was happening again. Happening worse than before. Her eyes narrowed, seemed to glaze over in that awful stare . . . but this time, instead of the usual panic, there was a new and fearful cruelty in them. Her mouth, teeth bared, curled up into that awful grimace. *"Ahhggghhh!"* she cried through the terrible grin. *"Ahhaaa!"*

I jumped back from her—I had seen that smile somewhere before!

Her hands held the art book open as if she'd just looked up from reading it. The grin was frozen on her face. Her eyes didn't blink. Behind her on my bedside table I could see my alarm clock: 7:27. I grabbed at the art book, but her fingers held it like a vise. I forced it away and flipped through the pages, backing across the room because she looked so . . . so much like the little evil face in the corner of Fitzgerald Cotton's later paintings! I dropped the book.

"No!" I cried, and I grabbed Mom's arm. She didn't blink, and she didn't unfreeze. "Mom, *no!*" It was like talking to a statue. The numbers on the clock changed, but nothing about Mom moved at all: 7:28.

The door to my room burst open and Crystal and Dad ran in. "We heard you yell," Crystal said. "Is it Mom—"

"Pam!" cried Dad, and he ran to her, gasping when he saw her ferocious face. "Oh, dear God!" he whispered, shuddering, and it really did sound like a prayer. "What is happening here?"

He bent over her as he had down in the kitchen and listened to her heartbeat. "It's very slow, kids; this is really bad. How can this be happening? I think we could lose her . . . Oh—we need help!"

"I'll call!" Crystal shrieked. "I'll call nine-one-one!" She turned to leave the room, looking back over her shoulder at Mom's evil grin and cold, glittering eyes. As Crystal ran out, the folded paper fluttered to the floor in her wake.

My dad was working on Mom, trying so desperately to help her, panic in his eyes. After a few seconds he jumped up again. "Watch her, Con," he cried. "We need an ambulance!" He raced out of the room after Crystal, and I was alone with Mom.

"*Aggghhh,*" Mom groaned in the voice of the damned. "*Aghhhaaa!*" Blood was seeping out of her hairline again—really starting to drip. Flinching, I reached out and touched her cheek—no, wait a minute—not blood. Something else. Something else red. Wet and sticky . . .

I rubbed my fingers together. Sniffed them in disbelief. Felt my stomach drop.

Not blood—but *paint.*

Then I knew that the help we needed couldn't come from an ambulance. Dr. Rhodes and all of modern medicine wouldn't be able to help my mom—I knew this in my gut. People did not leak paint. They just *didn't.* But here was Mom, frozen, groaning. And that book. And that paper on the floor.

I reached down and picked up the folded paper that Mom had tried to keep from me. The brittle page tingled in my hands as I unfolded it and stared down at a sketch of Mom sitting on thick grass, holding out her hand. Her smile was an invitation. I reached out a finger and touched the charcoal drawing, and a wave of cold rolled over me....

I went limp, felt myself falling, had to close my eyes against the strong, freezing wind that began to blow from somewhere very close—and somewhere very far away.

PART TWO

The Model

❧

He feeds upon her face by day and night...
—Christina Rossetti,
"In an Artist's Studio"

Padua, Italy. June 1479

The Smiler sharpened his dagger with short, brisk rubs against the stone. He smiled as he worked, a smile most unpleasant. He was thinking of how he had used this dagger in the past, and how he might use it again. The sharpening stone was actually the foot of a statue of Zeus, chiseled off and stolen from an ancient temple during one of Lorenzo's trips to Greece.

There came a gentle *tap-tap* on the heavy wooden door to his chamber. The Smiler slid the dagger back into its sheath strapped onto his leg and hidden by his cloak. *"Avanti!"* he called in his smooth, deep voice. The door opened to reveal a young woman. She slept—when he allowed her to sleep—in the small chamber above this tower room.

"Ah, my dear," he said. "You are always punctual." He returned her curtsy with a low bow, then led her into the room. He watched her with his acute artist's eye, enjoying the look of awe that flitted each morning across her beautiful face as she entered his well-appointed studio.

The studio was in the first room of the east tower, at the edge of the property he had inherited from his father. The stone walls of his studio were covered with fine tapestries worked in colors deep and bold. There were bowls of fresh fruits and urns of flowers, gathered each day by his servant, atop the round table. Shelves of canvases and paints lined the walls, and comfortable benches topped with brocade cushions waited by the fireplace. On this warm morning no fire was needed, so the grate was swept clean and filled with fragrant rosemary to scent the room.

"Come," the Smiler said to his model. "We must work while the light is right. Resume your position. And please do remove your hat"—he deftly unpinned the young woman's feathered concoction and lifted it away from her rich, chestnut hair—"like so. Yes, you know there's no need for outdoor clothing. Yet you continue to dress each morning as if you might be going out. Get it into your head, my beloved! You will not be leaving this place until I give you permission. And we are not yet finished with our work."

She lowered her eyes, but not before he saw the flash of—it would not *dare* be anger, would it?—some quickly veiled emotion. She knew by now to keep silent before him.

He offered her a sip of ale, then arranged her as he wanted her. The pose was the same as it had been for months, but as much as she professed to want to please him, she still needed him to set the pose.

Francesca. His family had known hers forever. He'd wanted her, as a boy, had asked for her hand in marriage—but she'd refused him. Refused the Smiler! And married someone else, and had a son. For years Lorenzo had not seen her, though he sent his spies out to keep watch over her and report back. Last year her husband had died and Lorenzo rejoiced—though it was too late to marry her himself. Lorenzo's father had pushed him into marriage years earlier with a paltry young girl of his father's own choosing. No matter. He rarely saw the girl. He lived to paint, and what he wanted to paint was the bride who had been denied him!

The poor widowed Francesca needed money now for herself and her young son. When Lorenzo's servants arrived with word that he would pay well to paint her, she agreed. Leaving her baby behind in the care of a nursemaid (paid for by Lorenzo—an unfortunate expense, but he didn't want the brat around while he worked on the mother), Francesca traveled to Padua.

Now she was finally *his*. The Smiler exulted every morning as he set her into the pose.

"Now, you must sit very still as always," he instructed

her, moving his easel to the correct position, close but not too close to his subject. "Head up—to the left, chin a bit higher, arms out—like so." He gave her the single rose to hold—a fresh one, of course, because they wilted so fast in the warm room. "Hold the flower in two fingers, up like this—perfect." He stood back and regarded her.

She was already drooping. *"Diàvolo!"* he hissed. She flinched. He snapped his fingers in front of her face. "You will keep your eyes on me! They must be fixed on me at all times, do you understand?" She had been growing more and more restless, talking to him about her baby or her dead husband. Sometimes Lorenzo had to shout at her. "You shall neither look away nor move at all. *Never* break your pose. Yes? Well then, are we ready to begin?"

She moistened her lips and murmured that she was trying, she always did try.... "Yes," she whispered, "I am ready."

"Very well, then," said Lorenzo da Padova, smiling his special smile. "We shall begin the day's work." He set about mixing his powdered pigments with fresh egg yolk, aware how uncomfortable she was in the pose, how it fatigued her muscles and dragged on her spirit as she struggled to hold it—and this entertained him. She was learning to discipline her mind and body to his will— and he enjoyed watching her. She wanted the money he promised when the portrait was finished, but he wanted much more from her. He wanted her very soul.

She had been quite satisfactory during the first month he had worked on the painting—excellent, in fact, at first, but then growing more vexing with time. Some days she could not seem to sit still. More than once she had fallen asleep, then jerked awake, and in doing so, upset the stand that held his bowls of paints. When that happened he would chastise her, of course. It was easy enough for such a skilled artist as himself to ignore the bruises that marred her face when he worked. On canvas she still looked bright and fresh, as lovely as the first day she'd stepped into his studio.

Now the clear morning light slanted through the small panes of glass at the narrow windows. Lorenzo's dagger rested lightly against his leg, hidden from view. His model watched him steadily, her gaze frightened but never wavering.

"*Perfetto,*" the Smiler whispered. "Perfect. You are so lovely. And now—*freeze.*"

✑ Chapter 6 ✑

Posing

When the wind finally stopped, I found myself lying all curled up, weak and tattered, like a piece of newspaper blown across the playground. It felt like I was waking up from a deep sleep. I wanted to stretch but was too tired and too heavy to move a single muscle. All the energy had been sucked right out of me. I lay completely limp, with a sort of sick feeling in my stomach. I felt the fuzz of rug scratch my cheek.

Then I smelled smoke.

Cautiously I lifted my heavy head. My eyes smarted as smoke puffed right in my face.

"Hold it right there, boy!" a man's gruff voice roared at me. "Don't move a muscle!" His face loomed in front of me. My stomach clenched. As I drew in a smoky breath, I remembered *everything:* Mom's tortured face, Dad's panic, the sketch—

Had the wind knocked me unconscious? I could see I wasn't in my bedroom anymore. And who was this man—maybe a doctor? But why would a doctor be puffing on a pipe? And where were Mom and Dad and Crystal?

I closed my eyes, dizzy again. My brain wasn't working right. In all that wind, my brain must have gotten rattled. Something had happened to me. But what?

I heard the man's voice in the fog. "That's good. Stay nice and still till I finish your face. Good, very good."

I opened my eyes again carefully. I could see that I was lying on a brown rug in an atticlike room, with streams of soft afternoon sunlight glinting through the open window. A warm breeze touched my face, and I smelled flowers. The breeze fluttered the cloth that covered a large canvas propped on an easel by the opposite window.

"All righty then, boy, turn your face toward me, just a bit to the right. There—just there! Perfect. Now hold it just like that!"

I obeyed the voice slowly, fear pumping adrenaline through me. *Who is this man?* Mom's eternal warning seemed to echo in my ears: *Stay away from strangers.*

"Lift your chin, and turn toward me, for crying out loud!"

I lifted my chin and looked over, holding my breath. All I saw was a tall, skinny guy standing by an easel. He had gray hair all over the place, like a mad scientist, but his face looked youngish—and he wore pants with red suspenders, and a white shirt with the sleeves rolled up. He was chewing on a pipe, puffing hard, and the smoke billowed around his head in a cloud. His face was creased with concentration, and he was dabbing at a canvas on his easel with a paintbrush.

"I've almost got it—just a little more blue right here," the painter said, and stabbed his brush into a jar of other brushes. "That's all for today." He clapped his hands at me. "All right, lad, get up and out of here—nap time's over! And next time you take it into your head to settle down for forty winks in my studio, let me know ahead of time so I can set up. It gave me a turn, I don't mind telling you, when I came in and saw you lying there like something the cat dragged in. I'd have preferred you to be over there on the sofa rather than beached like a dead fish on the floor—better lighting. And those clothes! I'd choose a different shirt." He frowned at me as I struggled to stand up. My legs felt as weak as if I had been scaling mountains.

"What's that mean, boy?" The man was scowling at my T-shirt. " 'Rolling Stones Revival'—that some kind of revival meeting? Are you one of them religious fellows going door-to-door proclaiming the Lord cometh?"

I glanced down at my shirt. "It—it's just an old rock group." My voice came out hoarse and raspy, as if I'd been sleeping for a long time. "My dad got me the shirt—"

"Rocks? Your dad is a geologist, is he? You must belong to that family on the next block. Heard the fellow teaches at the college."

Now that the fog was clearing, fear made me feel razor sharp. My head pounded with questions.

What was going on?

I took a deep breath and tried to be calm. Okay. Okay—this guy didn't *look* like an alien. And *he* didn't seem to know what was going on any more than I did; that was clear. While he stood there looking at me, my mind was ticking ahead, trying to figure out what I needed to do. *Run!* screamed some part of me, the part that was pumping adrenaline into my blood. *Stay cool,* whispered another part. *Look around. Figure out what's happened.* How had I come to be here, when moments ago I was in my bedroom with Mom—poor Mom—and looking at that sketch? ...

The sketch! It wasn't in my hand any longer. Where was it? I took a deep breath and looked around the studio—because that's what it was, an artist's studio. There were stacks of canvases along every wall, and shelves full of paints, jars of brushes, books and note-books. A table in the center of the room held clusters of shells, pottery, a toy dump truck, a bowl of eggs, and lots of other stuff. The windows didn't have any cur-tains, and the sunlight was streaming in. There was a skylight in the ceiling that sent more light down, like a beacon, across the floor.

"Next time you need a nap," the artist guy was say-ing to me sternly, "you ought to knock properly on the door, not just walk right in. It's only good manners! Are you a friend of Homer Junior? You look to be right about his age."

Homer Junior?

The artist's voice turned gruffer. "Cat got your tongue? Legs don't work, my boy? Come on now, get your bones outta here! I'm a workingman—or at least I'm trying to be."

I moved shakily toward the door. That's when I saw a calendar hanging from a nail on the wall near the sink. I edged toward it. It said MARCH 1926.

"'March 1926,'" I read, my voice still rusty. I felt like you do after a bad bout of flu—sort of shaky and faraway.

"April, actually," said the man, reaching over and ripping the sheet for March right off. He balled it up and tossed it toward an overflowing tin wastebasket in the corner. "Always forget to change the dang thing."

Nineteen twenty-six, nineteen twenty-six. The number kept repeating in my head.

I heard footsteps tapping up the stairs somewhere nearby. The door to the studio opened and an elderly woman stood there with a smile on her face and a dish towel in her hands.

"Hello, dear," she said in a surprised voice when she saw me. "Now, when did you come to call?"

"He just seems to have dropped in," replied the artist. "Chum of Homer's, no doubt. I wish you'd keep the children downstairs, Mother. How am I going to work with these disturbances?"

"I'm sorry, Fitz, dear," she replied. "But I see his appearance gave you something new to sketch. So that's good, isn't it?"

"I try to sketch whatever's to hand," he muttered. "Might as well. Now take him downstairs, would you?"

"Why don't you come down, too, dear? We're having

lemonade on the porch." Then she turned to me. "I'm Mrs. Cotton. My grandchildren and I are down on the porch, and you're very welcome to join us—"

Cotton? Like that guy in Mom's art book? I turned to the man. "Are . . . are you that painter? I mean, Fitzgerald Cotton?" My voice sounded weird. I tried again in a firmer voice. "I mean, you're the famous artist?"

"'Famous?'" He looked gratified. "At your service, lad. And always in need of people to sit for me, even if they don't knock before coming in. I do portraits mostly."

I was still trying to understand what seemed to be happening here. "You mean—" It couldn't be so, but I had to ask it, anyway. . . . "You mean, you're the painter in the art book? The one with the muse?"

In a flash the seemingly mild man turned into a raging tiger. He lunged, toppling me back down onto the floor. "WHO TOLD YOU ABOUT THAT?" he roared. His eyes blazed down into mine with a fiery intensity. "WHAT DO YOU KNOW ABOUT *HER*?"

I struggled to get him off me, but he was much stronger. He pinned my arms above my head with one big hand. The other hand grabbed the neck of my T-shirt. I thought he was going to hit me—or strangle me.

"Fitzy!" I heard his mother shout over the roar in my head.

"Tell me, young scoundrel, before I thrash it out of you!" the man yelled at me. "What do you know of her? Where is she? Where is my Pamela? TELL ME!" His voice rose with every word until he was shouting the house down. "TELL ME OR I'LL THROTTLE YOU!"

He knows Mom's name? I thought in terrified amaze-ment as I kicked him hard in the leg and heard him grunt with pain. But he didn't let me go. Then the woman, waving the dish towel over her head like a lasso, pushed herself between us.

"Fitzgerald!" she yelled. "Stop it this instant! My goodness gracious, what has gotten into you?" She pulled him away from me. Shakily I got to my feet. The maniac stood meekly aside as if he'd never done anything wrong in his whole life.

"Sorry, Mother," he said humbly. "I guess I just lost my temper."

"I guess so!" exclaimed the woman, dusting me off with her dish towel. "Now, are you all right, lad?"

"Not really," I said haltingly. *He knows Mom's name. He knows Mom's name!*

"He should be thoroughly ashamed of himself."

"I am ashamed, Mother. Indeed I am," said her son meekly. "The lad just—surprised me." Fitzgerald Cot-ton's words came out in a rush. "I thought he might know something about her. Or at least about a missing sketch of mine. One that is very dear to me. It's the one I did of Pamela—"

"I'm sure he wouldn't take any of your sketches," said Mrs. Cotton. "Would you, lad?" she asked me.

I shook my head. I was feeling dizzy again.

"Just a misunderstanding, then," the artist answered quickly in a mild, friendly voice. But the look he shot me was anything but mild or friendly. It was full of menace.

"He seems to be a good lad," continued Cotton in

the same fake voice. "Just moved in around the block, you see. Father's a geologist at the college...I'm hoping he'll come back and model for me. How about it, boy? Will you come back tomorrow and let me finish this sketch? Then I'll turn it into a portrait."

I didn't answer.

The woman looked at me with a frown. She started to say something, then thought better of it and pressed her lips together. She turned to her son. "Well, I hope you'll pay the lad for his time."

The man nodded his shaggy head. "Of course, Mother. I'll pay him handsomely! I'll pay him for his time today. A whole quarter. How about that?" He fished in his pockets. His hands were trembling as he pressed a coin into my palm. "Now, you be back here tomorrow morning sharp on the dot of nine, and we'll finish up the painting."

I just stared at him and started backing toward the door. I couldn't get my mind around what seemed to have happened to me—and the fact that this man knew my mom. How could any of this be real? A calendar that said 1926? A man with the same name as the artist from the big art book—attacking me? And now, the guy calm again, trying to arrange to paint me?

None of this made sense, and yet a little niggling throbbing in my head was telling me it did make sense, if only I could believe it. I rubbed my eyes, hard.

"You're looking tired, lad," the artist said in his deep, kind voice that nonetheless held the hint of menace. "So we'll talk again tomorrow—about all manner of things. Things that interest us both, my boy. How about that?"

I hesitated, my heart still thumping hard. I wanted to mention Mom again, and the sketch of her that made the wind start blowing, but I was afraid of what he'd do. And if the calendar on the wall was right, and this was 1926...

But of course it *couldn't* be. But what if it really was?

Time travel? A quick vision of Mom astride a brontosaurus flashed behind my eyes.

So the crazy artist was right about one thing: We definitely *did* need to talk. I needed to find out what was going on—and how I would get home again.

He shot out his hand, grabbing my arm. "Tomorrow, boy. How about it?"

There was a curious pleading note in his voice. I glanced down at the coin in my hand. It was a quarter. Slowly I held it up, squinted at the year: 1924. It felt hard and cold in my hand, and as real as anything.

Proof that this wasn't all some fantastic dream?

"All right," I whispered.

"Well, if you've got that settled," said Mrs. Cotton, "then why not come downstairs with me for that glass of lemonade?" She smiled kindly at me and tucked a long gray strand of hair back into the bun at the nape of her neck. "The children will want to meet you. If you've just moved here you've probably not met many playmates, I'll be bound."

"Thanks," I murmured, "ma'am." I don't think I'd

ever used the word *ma'am* in my life, but it seemed to come naturally now.

Then she spoke to her son. "You come on down and have a glass, too, Fitz."

He shook his shaggy head. "No, Mother. Not me." Then he looked straight at me. "Nine o'clock sharp?"

Without a word I sidled past him, out of the room. He didn't stop me.

As I started down the steep stairs, following Mrs. Cotton, I glanced back. Fitzgerald Cotton was still standing in the doorway of his studio, looking after me with hard, glittering eyes. I stared back at him, my eyes just as hard.

I felt baffled and threatened at the same time, but I would be back. And I wanted answers.

∾ Chapter 7 ∾

Cookies and Lemonade

I tried to catch my breath. *Okay, okay,* I told myself. *Relax.* Take a look around 1926. Try to figure things out.

Mrs. Cotton was leading me down a hallway lined with doors. I peeked inside the bedrooms as we passed them. The rooms were a lot smaller than the ones at my house, but the ceilings were high. The beds were all neatly made. Quite a lot of beds, it looked like, and one had stuffed animals and dolls heaped on it. All the window shades were half drawn against the sun outside, so the rooms were dim and quiet.

The last room was a bathroom with a funny clawfooted tub. "Excuse me," I said, stopping at the door.

"Come down when you're ready," Mrs. Cotton said. "The towel is clean."

I slipped into the bathroom and closed the door, leaning against it for a moment. I felt lost. Things were just *happening*—unplanned things. I didn't know the script for this movie. I didn't have a schedule of events for my time here—the way I have stuff written in my Day Planner at home to keep me on track with everything I'm supposed to do. And I had no special powers like I would if this really were a movie. Just to make sure, though, I pointed my finger at the sink. "Water!" I commanded. But of course nothing happened. *"Mom,"* I whispered into the mirror above the white porcelain sink. "Mom, I want to come home." I leaned forward and pressed my forehead against the mirror. It felt cool on my hot skin.

I felt like some sort of Goldilocks, sneaking around in the bears' house. *Fee-fi-fo-fum!* No, wrong story. That was Jack, up his beanstalk, hiding from the giant. I saw the video when I was little.

I took a deep breath and tried to push thoughts of bears and giants away. But the fact was that I was an intruder in this house. I really was like Goldilocks—or Jack. I tried to remember what had happened to them. I stared at myself in the mirror and wondered what would happen to *me*. My face looked so familiar—still the same, even in 1926. Same wild dumb curls, same greenish eyes, same weird nose.

I used the toilet, and when I finally figured out that you had to pull the long dangling chain hanging from a tank at the top to make it flush, I felt like I'd accomplished something great. I washed my hands and practically scalded myself because the sink had two taps, one cold and one hot, with no way to mix the water together to make warm—unless you put in the plug to fill up the whole sink. Before I left the room, I just had to sneak a peek into the mirrored medicine chest.

In *my* bathroom cupboards there are bottles of shampoo in bright colors and cream rinse with big plastic heads of cartoon characters. There's my musical electric toothbrush, some half-used-up tubes of toothpaste, and my retainer. And deodorant, Band-Aids, cotton balls, and this gross green mouthwash stuff Crystal gave me for my birthday. But here, in *this* bathroom medicine chest of 1926, there was only a little orange bottle labeled IODINE, a round box marked BEST TOOTH POWDER, and eight toothbrushes.

My heart started thudding hard because eight toothbrushes meant eight people. It hadn't sunk in when I'd seen all the beds, but now there were these toothbrushes...and now I could hear people in the house. There was music—a piano, played badly. There were running footsteps and a slamming door. A child shouting, "Hey, no throwing lemons!" And someone giggling wildly, high-pitched, like a maniac.

I pictured goblins hurling lemons at each other, like in some weird fairy tale.

I shut the door of the medicine chest carefully.

"Yoo-hoo!" called Mrs. Cotton's voice up the stairs, and I jumped back from the sink. Slowly I crossed the small room and opened the bathroom door.

"Coming," I squeaked. Then I tried for a normal voice. "Coming!" And I took a deep breath and headed out into the hall and down the last flight of stairs.

First thing I saw was a weird telephone on the wall in the hallway. It looked just like one I'd seen on a field trip to a museum once, without the display case.

I looked frantically around at the dimly lit hallway, the quiet rooms leading off it, the utterly unfamiliar spaces. I didn't know what house I was in, or what town or what state—or anything. I looked back at the telephone. I grabbed the horn and held it to my ear. My finger lifted, wanting buttons to punch. There weren't any. There wasn't even a dial tone, just a woman's nasal voice in my ear saying, "Your exchange, please?"

I didn't know what that meant. I said, very quietly, "I want to make a call. To California. Area code nine-two-five. The number is four-six-five-nine-six—"

I heard a nasal snort in my ear. Then the voice said again, "Your *exchange,* please."

"I'm trying to tell you the number!" I was whispering. But I suspected that no matter what number I asked for, it would never ring a phone at *my* house.

"Speak up, please, I cannot hear you..."

I knew somehow this wasn't going to work. But...it had to work! Telephones were our lifeline! I'd been taught from the minute I was old enough to remember: In an emergency, push 9-1-1.

Here there was nothing to push.

I took a deep breath, feeling like I couldn't get enough air in this place. But there *was* air—a breeze coming right in from the open front door. It smelled fresh, like lemons.

"We're out on the porch, dear," said the woman's voice from outside.

I hung the receiver gently back on the wall. Then I stuck one hand into my pants pocket to try to look casual—and I found Doug's key chain. I rubbed it for good luck as I opened the screen door and stepped out onto the porch of this old-fashioned house in 1926, somewhere in the world—if it was even the same world anymore.

I felt like Luke Skywalker entering the Death Star.

There were kids on the porch, and at first I couldn't even tell how many there were, the way they were running and leaping around and making so much noise. A frosty glass of lemonade appeared in front of my face, and a voice said, "Here you go, dear. Freshly squeezed."

A little boy careened past me. Mrs. Cotton clapped her hands at him and called out sharply, "Chester! Come over here and meet our new neighbor." Then she patted me on the shoulder. "This is Chester, my youngest and wildest grandchild. And what did you say your name was, dear?"

I took a deep breath, hesitating, thinking maybe telling her my name wasn't a good idea. But then I thought: *What can it hurt? I'm not even born yet.*

"I'm Connor," I told them. "Connor Chase." I gave the kid a little smile, all the while darting looks around me. The cars in the street were big and boxy and black, with skinny wheels and running boards. They looked like something right out of an old movie. There were a couple of houses across the street, with big porches like this one. Tears pricked behind my eyes, they really did, when I saw Mount Diablo rising above the hills, right in its usual spot. I was somehow so glad to see it. It meant that even if this was really 1926, at least I was on our own planet Earth, in America, in California—in Shady Grove, even.

I remembered something Mrs. White always said: *"Be grateful for small mercies."* I looked at the mountain and was very grateful.

If the familiar view of the mountain was anything to go by, then this 1926 house was standing where my house should be. Would one day be? I remembered my dad telling me how our whole housing development had been built on land that was an old neighborhood in a lemon grove. Here and now the wildfire that burned everything down was decades in the future, and the air still smelled of lemons.

"Say hello to Connor," the woman was telling the kids. She pointed at them one by one. "Connor, these wild things are my grandchildren. Betty is thirteen, and Homer is eleven. Elsie is nine, and Chester here is eight. And did I introduce myself? I'm Mabel Cotton—Mrs. Edgar Cotton. But never you mind asking *my* age!"

The bigger girl and the guy my age actually stuck out their hands for me to shake. Betty was a spindly kind of girl about as tall as Crystal. She wore her hair in a short bob, cut to her chin, with thick bangs in front. Homer, who was just my age, had dark hair slicked back from a neat center part. He wore round, wire Harry Potter–type glasses. The youngest kid, Chester, looked like a smaller version of Homer, but without the glasses. He had his hair parted and slicked back, too, and he had two big front teeth that stuck out a little and made him look like a chipmunk.

The girl called Elsie—she was the shocker. I sucked in my breath, feeling light-headed and strange. I needed to sit down fast in one of the white rocking chairs. I had seen Elsie before.

She was crossing her eyes and sticking out her tongue at me. This time she wasn't wearing the gigantic hair bow, but I recognized her just the same. She was the girl from the painting of *Elsie's Party, 1926.*

Whether I wanted to believe it or not, somehow I had traveled back in time. It was really 1926, and I was sitting here on the porch of the home of Fitzgerald Cotton, the man who had—somehow—painted so many pictures of my mom.

Okay, I told myself. *Be brave. There must be a way home again.*

I gave Elsie a weak smile, then sipped the lemonade. It was cold and soothing. "Hello," I mumbled.

"Hey, Connor," said Homer. "Where d'you live?"

"*Hay* is for horses, Homer," his big sister said primly. "Right, Gramma?"

"Shaddup, Betty," said Homer. He gave me a look that said, *Sisters!*

"Mind your manners, Homer," their grandmother said. "I must tell you, Connor, that I've met our new neighbors on the other block, and the husband is not a geologist at all. He is a professor of literature. He and his wife have no children, as far as I understand. Yet you told Fitz that you're their son?"

"Um, no," I said. "He just sort of came up with that himself. I never told him a thing."

"How odd. So—will you tell us? Where *do* you live?"

"Um . . ." I thought fast. "San Francisco?"

Betty snorted. "Are you asking us or telling us?"

"Telling you," I said firmly, warming up to the idea of creating a past for myself. Of course I couldn't tell them the truth. They'd never believe me, anyway. "I'm from San Francisco, but, um, my family isn't there now. I mean, I live on my own."

The kids' grandmother looked concerned. "Surely your parents haven't deserted you!"

"Not exactly," I said, trying to think quickly.

Elsie piped up excitedly: "It's just like what happened before! Connor just dropped out of the heavens, Gramma! We can find room for him, too, just like we did for Pammie."

For *Pammie*? It was very weird hearing Elsie say my mom's name like that. So—familiarly. As if she really knew Mom. Fitzgerald Cotton had known Mom's name, too. *"Where is she? Where is my Pamela?"* he had asked upstairs in the studio. What was happening? How could they know anything about my mom?

There had to be some connection between these people here in 1926 and Mom—and me. My mind was totally whirling, trying to get a grip on such bizarre thoughts, when I heard Mrs. Cotton's voice speaking urgently through the fog of my dizziness.

"So your parents have deserted you, Connor? And you are all alone in the world?"

"I—I'm an orphan." I invented hastily, stifling a quick stab of guilt at killing off my parents—even in a lie. "It's not too bad, most of the time. I manage all right." I stared down at the porch floor. "So I've been sort of traveling around looking for a job." Could kids work in this time? Seems to me I learned something once at school about how even little kids used to work in factories and mills and places like that in the olden times. But how old those olden times were, I had no idea.

When I looked up, the grandmother was staring at me. "You mean you actually have no one at all to look after you? No foster family? No guardian?"

"No—ma'am." My thoughts raced ahead. What if she took me to an orphanage or something? I needed to get back up to Fitzgerald Cotton's studio if I was going to figure out how to get home.

"Oh dear," Mrs. Cotton said thoughtfully.

"I would rather live on my own than in an orphanage," I said quickly, trying to sound competent and responsible. "I don't mind sleeping out in the streets—at least nobody's beating me. It's not too bad, really—except when I can't find any food. But I earn money by doing—um—odd jobs for people. Shining shoes and... um... running errands. And stuff."

Homer looked impressed. "What did you do when it was pouring rain the other night?"

"I slept under a parked car," I said, trying to look brave and needy at the same time.

It must have worked, because Chester, the youngest one, piped up, tugging on the woman's arm. "Gramma, we got room, don't we?"

The woman looked me over consideringly. "Yes, we can make the room. Connor? Would you like to stay here with us for a spell? Just until we work something out, of course—not the orphanage, don't worry. We'll find you someplace to stay."

"Oh yes, ma'am," I replied. "That would be really nice of you."

"You can sleep with Homer and Chester. We'll set up a camp bed."

"I sleep on a camp bed in my room with Mama and Betty," Elsie informed me, "and it's perfectly cozy and comfortable. And Pammie slept with us when she was here."

Pammie again! This was stranger than strange, but somehow I was starting to understand. I was in 1926. Mom had been here, too! But when? How could she have time-traveled and not had us notice she was gone? A trip to the past was something so weird, it would have to change a person in some way. I felt changed already, and I'd only just *arrived* here.

Then I remembered how different Mom was now. How much she'd changed.

She might have been here for a long time—and we'd never noticed. Because...how did time travel work?

Maybe she had been here and gone back—right to the very same moment she'd left. And so we never knew she'd been away! I could do the same thing—if only I figured out how to do it.

I felt I was holding some of the missing puzzle pieces in my hand. Things were weirder than ever, but somehow they were starting to make a little more sense.

"Will a camp bed be all right with you, dear?" pressed Mrs. Cotton.

"A camp bed will be great," I replied firmly. *I can do this,* I thought with a quick surge of excitement. I could take things as they came, and deal with them—and make it all up as I went along, with no one to arrange things for me. Sure, I was still scared. But—me! A time traveler!

I felt exhilarated and triumphant, like I was Doug's dad and had just scaled Mount Everest.

Betty was looking at me with thoughtful eyes. She looked at me like she could see right into my head. "What?" I said.

She made me nervous—and when she finally opened her mouth, I stiffened, expecting a challenge... something that might knock me off Mount Everest. But all she said was: "Nothing, really. It's just—you look so familiar. Like I've seen you before."

"Well, you haven't," I said firmly. But I knew I looked like Mom. Everybody said so. Should I tell her Pamela was my mother?

A voice inside me whispered, *Better wait.* So I decided I'd better take things slowly. Try to feel my way around until I could get home again.

The boys were setting up a board game on the big wicker footstool. "Want to play?" Homer asked me.

"Sure," I said. I mean, I figured if I could eventually return home to the same moment I left, then what was the hurry? Why not stay and *play*? "How do you play?"

They all stared at me as if I'd sprouted antlers or something. "Remember, he's an orphan," Elsie hissed.

"Ah, yes, our poor orphan," muttered Betty, meeting my eyes. I felt myself flushing red, and tensed again for a fight. But then she just shrugged and started explaining the rules.

Our game was called Snakes and Ladders. You moved your piece along the board and went up ladders if you were lucky. If you were unlucky you slid down slides (the snakes), then you had to basically start over. I had to start over three times, and Elsie thought that was hilarious. I hate losing games, but there was something fun, anyway, about sitting around on a nice afternoon with these kids. Only Chester wasn't playing. He was down in the grass doing something with a metal truck. Sometimes we heard him making soft *vrooom* noises.

"Hey, how come you guys aren't in school?" I asked them.

"Hay is for horses," said Betty sternly. She wasn't so different from Crystal after all.

"It's Easter vacation," Homer told me. "We get off all next week, too. Don't you go to school?"

I remembered my status as orphan on the run, and shrugged. "From time to time," I said airily. I glanced over to the kids' grandmother, hoping she wasn't listening. I really didn't want her thinking she had to contact the authorities or something. But she was smiling at another woman who was just coming up the path.

"Mama!" shouted Chester, and he jumped to his feet.

The kids' mom was a pretty woman, tall and slim, wearing a light green dress with beads shimmering on the skirt in the same style Mom had worn the day I first saw her with that art book. Even though the day was warm, this woman was wearing a hat. She took it off as she climbed the porch steps, and I saw she wore her dark hair curling softly against her cheeks like the girls did— and Mom did. Obviously this was a really trendy style, because only the grandmother wore hers differently, pulled back in a perfect old-lady bun. It's not like I go around noticing what people wear and what sort of hair they have—not usually, I mean. But here and now everything seemed worth noticing.

She set down her two large shopping bags and hugged Chester. "Hello, my pet. I see we've got company." Homer and Betty jumped up from the game and went to help carry the bags. They didn't even have to be asked, which was kind of weird but impressive. You wouldn't see that happening at my house—but then again, Mrs. White does all the food shopping, and part of her job is to bring the stuff in from the van and put it all away in the kitchen. Then I remembered, we *used* to have Mrs. White. I'd probably be doing a lot of fetching and carrying from now on. That is, when I went back.

"I'm Joanna Cotton," the woman introduced herself, holding out her hand to me. "I see you've met my brood of chicks."

"Hello," I mumbled, shaking her hand. Looking closer, I thought I recognized her from one of the paintings in the old art book, but I wasn't sure. "Yes, I've met everybody." I felt sort of tongue-tied. I remembered reading something about Fitzgerald Cotton's brother getting killed in some war. This must be his widow, and she and their children lived in the grandparents' house.

While Joanna and Mrs. Cotton went into the house with the groceries, the kids took me on a tour around the yard. Elsie hung on my hand and skipped along, dragging me with her. "Are you gonna stay forever, Connor? Are you gonna be our new brother?"

"No," I told her. "But I'll stay for a while."

Things seemed so fresh and comfortable, I had to be careful—otherwise I might get to feel too welcome here. I might forget I needed to find a way home.

The sketch was the key. I knew this instinctively. And Fitzgerald Cotton knew something about it. I would wait till tomorrow and ask him then—and search the studio, somehow. Nine o'clock sharp.

The kids showed me around their property. As far as I could tell, their house was on the exact same piece of land ours was built on—but it had a much larger yard than we had, and was all full of lemon trees. That field was, I guessed, the space where Doug's house would one day be built next door. It was an unsettling notion, really, that my house didn't even exist—that nobody in my whole family had been born yet—and here I was, walking right over the spot where a fire would rage—and where Doug and I would one day in the future be hanging out, playing PlayStation.

A rickety white picket fence surrounded the Cottons' property, and behind the house there was an old stable, but no horses. Homer told me he was hoping they'd get an *automobile* someday, and they would keep it in the stable. In the backyard there was a humongous vegetable garden in one corner. They'd planted all sorts of early crops, and I could see lettuces and cabbages and other stuff I didn't even recognize. *Our* vegetables came nicely trimmed, labeled, and wrapped in plastic.

All the kids were just standing there, looking at me as if they could tell I wasn't from around here.

"What?" I said. They made me nervous, staring like that.

"Where'd you get those duds?"

"What duds?" What *are* duds?

The kids all laughed—especially Homer. He was the one I'd heard laughing from upstairs, the one who sounded like a maniac goblin.

"Guess they have other words for clothing over in San Francisco," said Betty with a smirk. But she gave me a long look like maybe she suspected I wasn't really from San Francisco at all. Which of course I wasn't. "Your shoes—well. Never mind," she said.

I just shrugged. Back in my own time these shoes

were the coolest thing in the whole middle school. But it wasn't worth discussing my *duds*. There were more pressing things on my mind. "Um, about your uncle," I said.

"You've met him? Where?" Betty's eyes were wide.

"Um—up in his studio," I stammered.

"He never lets *us* up there." Her voice was challenging.

"I was posing for a portrait," I said. "But he got really...weird. Mean."

"Mama says he's a hot-blooded, hotheaded artist," said Homer. "As if that's any excuse. He's just plain grumpy."

Betty sighed. "He is grumpy these days," she agreed. "But he wasn't always like that. You kids don't remember him any other way, but I do. He takes things hard, Mama says. For years he felt guilty that our father died in the war." She sank down onto the grass near the garden and stared up at the blue sky. "Uncle Fitzy was exempted from battle because he had rheumatic fever as a child and it weakened his heart," she told me. "He's not supposed to exert himself or he could die."

"But our father was strong, and he did go off to fight in the Great War," Homer said sadly, "and so *he* was the one who died."

I sat down next to Betty on the grass. It was damp and cold on the ground, but the sun was warm on my face. "I'm sorry about your dad," I said. "That's really tough."

"Well, you know how it is," she said. But again there was that challenging note in her voice, like, did I *really* know?

"So we're nearly orphans, too," said Elsie mournfully.

"Chester and Elsie never knew him," Betty told me. She plucked some blades of grass and rolled them into a little green ball. "But I was five, and Homer was three, and I remember. Our dad didn't actually die in the war, not really. He came home wounded, and I remember how we all tiptoed around the house a lot, not wanting to disturb his rest. And the doctor was always coming by. For a while it seemed he was getting better. It was a chest wound, and he was weak, but he could sit up in a chair during the day, and even walk out here in the garden." She ducked her head and her hair hid her face. Her voice faltered. "But then he developed pneumonia, and he... he died, anyway."

"That's really sad," I said. It made me uncomfortable, listening to them talk about their dead dad. I mean, I know plenty of kids whose parents are divorced, but only one with a dead parent. That's Lissie Albertson, whose mom got hit by a car when she was crossing the street. Everybody feels so terrible for Lissie, but nobody knows what to say about her mom.

They were all silent for a second. Betty cleared her throat hard a few times.

"I remember Daddy, too!" insisted Elsie.

"You couldn't!" objected Betty, raising her head to frown at her sister. "You were only a one-year-old baby—and Chester wasn't even born yet."

"I was *almost* born!" said Chester indignantly.

"So your uncle's been in a bad mood ever since your dad died?" I looked around at the four kids. "And painting can't help him feel better? You know, like therapy?"

"Nothing made him feel better," said Betty. "Until Pammie came."

I got that weird, sick sort of feeling in my stomach again. "Tell me about her," I said, trying to sound casual.

"No, Connor," said Betty. "How about *you* tell us about her?"

I'd been expecting a challenge—but not this one, coming out of the blue like that. I was shocked. How had Betty guessed? The other kids hadn't, from the look of them. They were gaping at me and Betty in surprise. Obviously they hadn't cottoned on to it yet. *Cottoned* on to it. Get it?

"I don't know what you mean," I said sternly to Betty.

"Oh, of course," she replied. "You never heard of Pammie in your life?"

"How could he?" asked Homer.

"This is the exact spot where Uncle Fitzy found her," Elsie said suddenly. "Right, Homer? Wasn't it right here under the plum trees?"

"Yup." He nodded. "Lying on the ground like some old *corpse*—but she was only sleeping."

"He *found* her out here?" I asked. Mom must have been swept through the wind like I was. She must have landed here—just like I landed on the floor of the studio.

"Yup," said Elsie. "Right here." She sighed. "I miss her. I thought they were gonna get married. I coulda been the flower girl. It's not fair."

"What did you say?" I demanded. *"Married?"*

They just stared at me. I wrenched out a handful of

grass. "Who was going to get married?" I asked Elsie more gently, staring at the blades and dirt in my palm.

"Uncle Fitzy and Pammie, of course," Elsie said. "Pammie was Uncle Fitzy's model. He loved her; you could tell. But then she left us, and now we're all sad."

"Mama's not *so* sad," Homer corrected Elsie. "I mean, she liked Pammie and all—who wouldn't? But she'd rather have Uncle Fitzy marry *her,* don't you think?" He jumped high to pull down a tiny hard plum off the tree, and then looked over at me. "Since our dad's dead, our mama could get married again, you know. If she found the right person."

"Uncle Fitzy isn't going to marry Mama," said Betty scornfully. "He's in such a black mood all the time, he doesn't even notice Mama anymore. He doesn't notice *anybody* anymore, and he's grown rather horrid, if you ask me, even worse than before. He's always snapping at you when you say anything. I'm glad Mama won't be marrying such a grouch."

"He's just missing Pammie," said Elsie. "It's so romantic."

"*Hmmph.*" Betty sniffed. "If you like him so much, then *you* can take up his meal trays."

"I didn't say I like him!" Elsie corrected her hastily. "I just said he's missing Pammie."

I couldn't hold it in anymore. "Well, she couldn't marry him, anyway, because she's *already* married!" I blurted out. And then, of course, I wished I hadn't said it, because Homer and Elsie and Chester were all over me: "What do you mean?" "How could you know?" "Do you know Pammie after all?" and so on.

Betty just sat there with a superior smile on her face because I'd given myself away. She'd been right all along that I did know Pammie.

But I tried to cover up, anyway. "It's just an educated guess," I said quickly. "Probably that's why she left you—she must have had a husband waiting." I looked up at the lacy branches of the plum trees.

Here on this sun-warmed grass, my mother had been found by Fitzgerald Cotton. She'd been a time traveler just as I was—and to this same place. This was where she'd been and why she'd made that strange comment about having been away for so long! She'd known these same people I was just meeting now. It was more mind-boggling than any *Mad Scientist* episode I'd ever seen, because things like this just didn't happen.

But it had, and I couldn't help but feel it had happened for a reason. I was here because I was supposed to do something.

But what, Mom? Why didn't you tell me?

Because she couldn't. Because she was frozen. Maybe because she thought no one would believe her. I felt close to her suddenly, and almost thought I could hear her voice calling to me from far away.

Connor! Connor! The voice had a desperate tone to it.

I shook my head and the voice was gone. I looked up at all the kids staring at me and rubbed my hands across my face. "So tell me more about this model," I said to the kids in what I hoped was a cool, casual tone. "Like, did she just hang out here and get painted all the time? Didn't she have other stuff to do with her time— you know, like go to work? Didn't she miss her husband and children and job?"

Homer threw a small, unripe plum at me. "She never mentioned a husband or children. She stayed with us all year—and then just all of a sudden was gone. She's been gone about a month already, and Uncle Fitz has turned into a beast."

She was here a whole year? Hadn't she missed us? The thought made me uncomfortable. Hadn't she tried to come home?

"Why did she stay so long?" I asked.

"Why wouldn't she stay?" replied Homer. "She was Uncle Fitzy's best model."

Simple as that, huh? "But where had she come from in the first place?" I persisted.

"That's definitely one of life's big mysteries," replied Betty, raising her eyebrows at me. "And there are others. Maybe *you* can give us some answers?"

I had to look away from her again.

"Uncle Fitzy had a tantrum when Pammie left," Elsie reported solemnly. "A very big one. And he *keeps* having tantrums and crying about her. He needed her, and he loved her, and now he can't paint since she's been gone."

"He says he may never be able to paint again," added Homer. "He just stays up in his studio, raging and banging things around. Mama says it must feel like being in a black hole for him to be without his muse. Nobody can talk to him, and nobody but Gramma dares to get too near him." He threw another plum hard against the garden gate. "The old cuss."

Elsie had pulled up some little daisies and was threading the stems together in a daisy chain. "But it's not just Uncle Fitzy. We *all* miss Pammie—she was hotsy-totsy. She was the bee's knees." Then she added softly, "You would have liked her, Connor."

I looked up. Betty was still watching me.

∾ Chapter 8 ∾

The Paint Box

A bell started ringing somewhere, and all four of the Cotton kids jumped up. *Saved,* I thought. Betty made me nervous.

"Dinnertime!" yelled Chester, racing off for the house. "Grandpa's home!"

The rest of us followed. Grandpa was a round old guy, standing on the back stoop, waving a big handbell up and down. Suspenders held up his baggy brown pants, and he had a bald head like a shiny egg. Homer introduced him to me as Mr. Edgar Cotton. Mr. Cotton smiled and pumped my hand like he was trying to draw water from a well. Then we all went inside to the dining room.

This is what Mom wanted. The big round table was set for eight. There was candlelight. There were platters of chicken and potatoes and green beans with onions. I was seated between Homer and Betty, and I watched them out of the corner of my eye so I would be sure not to make any mistakes. The whole family—minus Uncle Fitzy, who apparently never came downstairs for meals and was served on a tray up in his studio—bowed their heads and said a prayer together. *Grace,* Mom had called it. *For what we are about to receive, may the Lord make us truly thankful. Amen.*

Then Mr. Cotton cleared his throat and said, "And, Lord, please end this blasted Prohibition so we can enjoy a glass of wine with our meal again! I have half a mind to turn bootlegger myself!"

"Now, Edgar," reproved Joanna. "It's the law."

"Damnable silly law, when the government tells us what to eat and drink in our own homes!" But he subsided and took a big drink of his lemonade.

I remembered how Mom had spoken of Prohibition at our dinner table. And with a shiver it hit me again that Mom had sat right here at this table with this family. Maybe she had sat in this very chair, where I was sitting now. Weird as that thought was, it made me feel safer somehow, like she was watching over me.

Mrs. Cotton started passing the platters, and that got my mind off Mom. Joanna had to help Chester, who was trying to take all the chicken for himself, and Mr. Cotton heaped green beans on my plate before I could tell him I really didn't eat green things. But everything smelled fantastic, anyway. And with the old man's blue eyes fixed on me, I couldn't very well not take a bite of the beans... which was when I found out I liked green things after all, at least in 1926. If Mrs. White would use real butter and lots of salt instead of nonfat yogurt and sprinklings of herbs on vegetables, maybe I'd eat them in my own time, too.

"Me first, me first!" shouted Chester all of a sudden, raising his hand like we were in school.

"No, you were first last time, Chess," Homer objected.

"Oldest to youngest," said Betty officiously. "That means I go first."

"Uh-uh," objected Elsie. "That would be Grandpa!"

Of course I didn't have a clue what they were talking about. But Joanna smiled. "Let's let our guest go first," she said, and turned to me. "Telling about our day. What were the high points of your day, Connor?"

Joanna went on to explain that this is what they always did at dinner, every night: listened to each other tell a few of the high points—or low points—of their day. *Copycat, Mom!* I thought.

"Uncle Fitzy used to eat with us," Elsie added, "and he always told us about how well his paintings were coming because Pammie was modeling."

"And what did...um...Pammie tell?" I asked.

"Oh, she loved to tell all sorts of things. About canning peaches with Mama," said Elsie. "Or learning to knit. Funny, there were a lot of ordinary things she didn't know how to do when she came. We figure she was probably very wealthy and grew up with lots of servants."

"But she was a fast learner," said Mrs. Cotton. "She was clever, our Pamela. Clever and mysterious, but what I wouldn't give for her to come back to us if it meant Fitz would be part of the family again." There was a really sad tone to her voice, and Mr. Cotton heard it, too.

"Now, Mother," he said gently, "let's not season our supper with tears. Let's hear from our new visitor. Can you tell us something cheerful, lad?"

I cleared my throat. "Well," I said, wondering what they'd say if I told them what really had happened to me today. Instead I looked around at all their interested faces and thought of what an orphan would say. "Well, my high point was dropping in on the Cotton family. It's so nice of you to let me stay. And to feed me! Definitely a high point." And I took a big mouthful of chicken so I wouldn't have to say anything else.

We went around the table, and everyone had something to say. And it *was* interesting, somehow, even though everybody said pretty much the same thing about how nice it was that I'd come to visit. But they added other high points, like Elsie's doll tea party in her friend Agnes's garden, and Betty's roller-skating race with her chums (that was her word: *chums*!) to the park and back, and Homer's and Chester's baseball game on the vacant lot. Joanna told about her shopping, and how she'd met up with Mr. Riley again, and how he'd said he'd like to call on her sometime.

"Not him again!" muttered Betty, but only I, sitting right next to her, heard. Or at least no one let on that they'd heard.

Mrs. Cotton told about her spring-cleaning and how she'd found three dollars and forty cents in change under various beds and chairs, and that she was going to use the money to buy herself a new hat.

Mr. Cotton told about his day at work. He was a

cabinetmaker with a small office on the main street of Shady Grove, where people came to order cupboards and bookshelves and tables and other things for their homes. Then he'd come home and make the furnishings out in the old stable behind the house. He always had more business than he knew what to do with, and now he was thinking of hiring someone to help out.

"Your Mr. Riley would like some extra work," he told Joanna.

"He's not *her* Mr. Riley!" muttered Betty under her breath.

Joanna stood and started clearing dishes. Mrs. Cotton rose from her chair and went to the kitchen, coming back a few moments later with a big chocolate cake. Everyone clamored for dessert, and after dinner was over, the kids' grandpa did some card tricks. They were great—"amazing feats," he called them. I begged him to show me how he did some of them, but he said it was magic. Homer hooted that there was no such thing, and Elsie screeched that there was so. Mr. Cotton just laughed and said a good magician never tells.

Joanna and Mrs. Cotton made me up a nice cozy bed in Homer and Chester's room. They found me a pair of Mr. Cotton's pajamas and rolled up the cuffs. Then Joanna tucked me in just like she did her own boys, and even dropped a kiss lightly onto my forehead. *Copycat, Mom!* I thought for the second time that evening. But I sort of liked what Mom was copying from the Cottons.

I liked Joanna's kiss. It made me feel safe for a moment, at a time when I was full of worries. I wondered whether this was how Mom had felt at the Cottons' house—safe and cozy and peaceful. If so, I could see how it would be easy for Mom to enjoy staying here. *But for a whole year, Mom? Weren't we worth coming back to?*

When their mom had gone downstairs, Homer and Chester started bombarding me with questions about what it was like being an orphan, my life on the mean streets, and everything. I just lay there because I didn't have the heart to invent a good story. I wanted to go to sleep so I could wake up and try to find my way home from this place. But they kept pestering. Finally I propped myself up on one elbow and looked across the room at them.

"You guys want a bedtime story?" I asked, keeping my voice soft. "Better than a sad tale of an orphan?"

They did.

"Okay, then, here's my favorite story. It's one of your basic fairy tales—only better. The eternal fight between good and evil." I knew just where to begin. "Long, long ago," I whispered dramatically, "in a galaxy far, far away..."

The story of Luke Skywalker and Darth Vader carried them both off to sleep, but I lay awake for a while longer, thinking about what had happened to me and how far away from home I was. Over and over in my head I saw Mom's last, frozen grimace before I grabbed the sketch. I remembered how I touched the drawing of Mom and went spinning through that cold wind—through time.

I lay there planning how I would search the art studio in the morning to find the sketch. Then I drifted into sleep, and I dreamed that my narrow little camp bed was a starship.

❧

I woke up to an earthquake. At least that's what I was thinking as my eyes flew open and I sat bolt upright. But it wasn't an earthquake. Just Homer and Chester, leaping from bed to bed to bed. I wasn't sure my little camp bed could stand the strain, so I got up. Homer led the way down the stairs. Just like at dinner everybody but Fitz ate breakfast all together. There was hot oatmeal to start the meal, then fluffy scrambled eggs, thick slices of bacon, piles of toast, and butter and jam. Everything was totally delicious, and much tastier than the Blueberry Twirls that Ashleigh gives us.

The whole time I ate, I kept trying to forget that I had an appointment with Fitzgerald Cotton at 9:00. It was one thing to plan how I'd search for the sketch up in the studio, and another to know there was a wild artist up there who had jumped me yesterday. I listened to the family's conversation. It was amazing how much they had to say—as if anything interesting could have happened to them overnight. But this time they weren't telling their high points; they were talking about magic. Homer started it all by asking his grandpa for some more magic tricks, and Mr. Cotton laughingly reminded him he'd said only last night there was no such thing as magic.

"Do *you* believe in magic, Connor?" Mr. Cotton asked, turning to me.

I swallowed my egg and wiped my mouth politely

with the cloth napkin before answering. "Absolutely," I replied, looking around me at all their faces. "I absolutely do believe in magic." And that was totally true, even though if you'd asked me only two days ago, I would have laughed you right out of town.

Betty kicked me under the table, but I didn't look at her.

"I don't think there's magic," Homer announced, "and if you want to know, I'll tell you why! Because if there was magic, then Daddy could have magicked away the bullets that hit him. Then his lungs wouldn't have been weak, and he wouldn't have gotten pneumonia."

"If I had a magic potion, I'd bring Daddy back to life," said Elsie.

I remembered how Crystal had pneumonia two winters ago. It started like a cold in her nose, then sort of sank into her chest, and then became a cough and wheezing. She had to stay home from school for a few days and take antibiotics, and then she was fine. "Antibiotics are sort of like magic potions," I told Elsie. "But they can't cure everybody every time, I guess."

"Anti-whats?" asked Homer with interest, but I shut my mouth quick in case there weren't any such things as antibiotics yet. "Maybe that's what Daddy needed, Mama. Anti-whatever pills."

"Anti-bullet pills, that's what he needed," said Elsie. "Anti-war pills."

Everybody was quiet for a moment. Betty picked up her grandpa's deck of playing cards and shuffled them in her thin fingers. "The rest of you can hardly remember

Daddy," she said. "But I do—and I know that Daddy believed in magic. His tricks were just as good as yours, Grandpa! He should have been a magician—not a soldier."

"I taught him all the tricks I knew, on his twenty-first birthday," Mr. Cotton said with a little smile. He turned his coffee cup around and around in his hands. "A special initiation."

"He was a bright spot in all our lives," Mrs. Cotton said, and for a second I was afraid she was going to cry or something. But she didn't. She looked around the table at her family and said, "But he left us something magical behind."

"He left you children and your mama," said Mr. Cotton in a husky voice.

"Fitzy always had such obvious talents," continued Mrs. Cotton musingly. "He had his gift for painting, from a very young age. But Homer had heart." She shook her head slowly, remembering. "He had a real good heart."

Joanna reached over and squeezed Mrs. Cotton's hand. "I remember Homer always said that happy families make their own magic," she said. "And I think he was right."

"Can I have some more bacon?" asked Elsie, and that was the end of the conversation. Even though it had been sort of a sad conversation, it was still interesting. We didn't have enough time, somehow, for conversations in my family.

Mr. Cotton put on his hat after he'd finished his

breakfast, and said good-bye. Then he left the house to walk to the streetcar that would take him to Main Street. And Mrs. Cotton said to all us kids, "So what are your plans for the day, kiddiwinks?"

It amazed me how they didn't have anything already set. They lived without schedules and were more responsible for filling their own days than any kids I knew. The thought of a whole day—a whole week of vacation with nothing in the Day Planner—made me sort of uneasy.

But the *"kiddiwinks"* were all full of ideas: Go to the candy store, play dolls, roller-skate to the candy store, read a book, take the dolls along in the wagon to the candy store...

It all sounded good to me. I sort of wished I'd never made my nine o'clock appointment. But if I didn't confront the beast in his lair, then I'd never get home again.

I pushed my chair back from the table so fast it nearly tipped over.

Joanna just smiled at me and said, "All right, the lot of you. Out to play! Gramma and I have a lot of work to do, and we don't want to see you around this kitchen until we ring the lunch bell." Her voice was brisk, but her smile was kind. "One, two, three *skidoo*!" Then she and Mrs. Cotton left the room.

Mom had probably worked in the mornings with Mrs. Cotton and Joanna, chatting the whole time they did spring-cleaning or cooking or whatever. *Somebody* had taught Mom to cook, after all. Or maybe she had modeled for Fitzgerald Cotton in the mornings and worked in the afternoons. Whatever.

I walked with the kids out onto the front porch. Nobody had warned them about staying near the house or keeping out of traffic or watching out for strangers, and none of the kids objected to being sent outside to play the way kids would in *my* neighborhood.

Betty grabbed Elsie's hand and said, "Run and get your paper dolls, and I'll help you cut out more clothes for them. We can sit here on the porch."

You'd never catch Crystal playing with paper dolls where anybody could see her, even though she and Betty were the same age.

And Homer said to me, "Hey, Con, wanna help me and Chess build a tree fort? Grandpa has loads of scraps of wood out in the stable we can use."

That sounded fun. But the big clock in the front hallway said 9:00 now. "I have a better idea, Homeboy," I said casually. "How about we all go up to your uncle's studio?"

"What's that you called me?" he asked, balling up his fists like he was going to deck me.

Whoa! "It's just a nickname," I told him quickly. "Like you called me 'Con.' And you call Chester 'Chess.' Nicknames sound friendly. I was just being friendly and asking you to come up to your uncle's studio."

"Oh." Homer relaxed his fighting stance. "I don't have a nickname," he said. "Everybody else does, but I don't."

"That's why I thought I'd call you Homeboy. It means, like, you're one of the gang. But if you like Homer better, hey, I'll call you Homer. No problem. I could even call you Homer *Junior* if you want to be formal."

He was balling up his fists again. "Don't you dare!"

"Sorry! Just plain Homer. Homer is a great name." Actually I thought Homer was a really dorky name. "Anyway, *Homer*," I continued, "what about it? I'm supposed to model for your uncle." It was the only appointment in my Day Planner for 1926. "Want to come with me?"

"Not in this lifetime," Homer said, shaking his head. "Uncle Fitzy is a grouch. You go on your own, and when he's done with you, come out to the big tree in the back. Chess and I will be working on our fort."

When he was done with me? I didn't like the sound of that. I turned to go inside. But when Homer called my name, I turned back.

"Hey...Con? Maybe I could get to like that nickname. You know, *Homeboy*. It's the bee's knees." He waited a second, but I didn't answer right away. He called again: "Hey, Con?"

"Hay is for horses, Homeboy," I shot back, and he laughed. Then he and Chess went down the porch steps. I closed the front door, suddenly all alone.

I thought about magic as I climbed the stairs to the third floor. If happy families made their own wonderful magic, as Homer Senior had believed, then did it follow that unhappy people like Fitzgerald Cotton made their own *terrible* magic? Their own *black magic*?

Taking a big breath, I rapped on the door at the top of the stairs.

"Go away!" boomed Fitz's voice. "Get out of here, whoever you are! I don't want coffee and I don't want tea and I don't want your blasted lemonade! If you have any proper whiskey, there might be something to talk about—but if not, then stay out!" There was a crash, like a pile of canvases tipping over. There came another crash and the sound of shattering glass. "Where is my muse?" The voice rose to a shout. "Answer me *that*!" Another bang, another crash, as if the maniac behind the door was throwing his brushes and paint pots around. "I tell you, it's not working anymore, that's all there is to it—and I'm going to sit up here the rest of my life until I get it right. And if I never get it right, then I'll be here until my corpse is a moldering, stinking heap on the floor!"

I guessed it would be okay after all to go out with the boys and build the fort. But just as I was turning away, there came another crash that made me jump, and then a howl.

"Pamela, my angel, you *will* come back to me! You *must*—and you SHALL!"

At the sound of that crazy man's voice calling my mom's name, I bashed open the door so hard that it slammed against the wall. I gasped at what I saw.

There was Fitzgerald Cotton, still in his bathrobe, standing in the center of the room under the skylight, holding a paintbrush. His wild grayish hair stood up in tufts. Light streamed in from the skylight and lit up the whole studio. Piles of canvases had been knocked over onto the floor, as well as chairs, paint pots, glass jars holding pencils and extra brushes, stacks of magazines, a small table, and an easel. The place was trashed.

"Oh no," I said. "Oh no, oh no, you don't!" I wasn't talking about the mess in the room. I was looking at the painting on the big canvas under the skylight.

There was Mom. Painted on the canvas. Frozen in the exact terrible pose she'd been in when I'd grabbed the sketch. Her mouth was stretched in a scream. Her eyes were wide, the pupils distorted. The eyes seemed to be looking at me—not staring blankly but imploring me to help. There were dabs of fresh paint along her cheekbones.

I stared in shock at the painting, feeling as frozen as she had been last time I saw her. Mom looked so alive on the canvas, and so frightened. Then I unfroze and raced to the easel.

"Get back!" snarled Fitzgerald Cotton, taking a step toward me. "This is going to be my masterpiece, and I don't want anybody near it."

"Masterpiece?" I cried. "It's *horrible*! Why are you painting her like *that*?"

"I know it's not my best work—yet—but it will be! It must be! With her gone, I'm painting only from memory, and I can't get it right now, no matter how hard I try. But I'll *never* stop trying! Get out of here, boy—don't distract me from my work!"

"Stop painting her!" I shouted back. "Just leave her alone!" How could he see into the future to know how Mom looked when she was frozen? How could he know to paint her with that horrifying face?

Then it hit me. She was frozen because he *was* painting her. Because he was making her *pose* for him. "No," I whispered. "Stop."

There was silence all of a sudden in the studio. Absolute silence. Then Fitzgerald Cotton cleared his throat. "You must tell me what you know of her, boy."

I sucked in a deep breath and glanced behind me to make sure the door to the room was still standing open. No way was I going to be locked in here with this guy. "I know that's one unhappy model," I said as I pointed to the big canvas, where Mom was terrified, trapped, helpless. "You're *killing* her."

Fitzgerald Cotton turned back to the canvas. He studied it. I waited in silence, wanting like anything to scream at him that this was my mother, and he'd better stop tormenting her, or else—or else! Or else what? I couldn't think what. And I couldn't think what he'd do to me if I said she was my mother.

"I *must* paint her!" He daubed a little paint onto Mom's face, then he growled low in his throat like a wolf or some other wild creature. "She wants me to paint her! You know, boy, how the eyes of portraits often seem to follow the viewer? It's an illusion, of course—usually. But *her* eyes really do follow me. They're begging me to paint her."

"I think they're begging you to *stop* painting her!" I returned in as steady a voice as I could manage—not very steady at all, really. This was one scary guy.

"I just can't get the face right anymore," he whispered. "She was so easy to paint while she was here—so lovely. I don't know why I'm remembering her now like *this*! Every time I've tried to paint her since she left me, from memory, I get *this*!" He swept his arm toward the easel.

I ventured: "It's obvious, isn't it, from the way she looks, that she's gone off to some faraway place and she doesn't *want* you to paint her anymore!"

He didn't seem to hear me. He dotted more paint onto Mom's face. "Look! It's rubbish. Even with my most special paints—I just can't capture her now."

Oh, but he *was* capturing her, big time. Could he really not know it?

I scrubbed my fingers through my hair, trying to think. My mom had arrived here—somehow. This guy had painted my mom while she was here—I knew *that* from seeing the pictures in the art book and from what the kids had told me. He called her his muse, his inspiration. Had he held her captive? He must have somehow, I told myself firmly. Or else Mom wouldn't have stayed a full year in this place.

But then Mom had come home to us—escaped?— somehow. And so Fitzgerald Cotton lost his muse and had to paint her from memory. But...

Here I felt lost. Because I couldn't figure out why his painting Mom from memory should make her look like such a monster.

Fitzgerald Cotton was watching me closely. He pushed his wild hair out of his eyes and took a deep breath, like he was trying to calm himself. Then he seemed to relax. He reached out a big hand and cupped my face.

"You look like her, you really do. I saw it yesterday. That's why I want to paint you. Are you related? You must be! Same big green eyes. Same fair curls. Same little chin—" His fingers tightened, and kept on tightening. I jerked my head away.

"All right," I said, not answering any of his questions. "Fine. Go ahead and paint me. Just stop painting *her*."

He turned away and scooped up some of the fallen brushes. "Yes, could be it will calm me to have a change of subject. I get so agitated, thinking of her, my mysterious Pamela."

Again it was on the tip of my tongue to tell him she was no mystery, she was my mom. I wanted to *claim* her. But his face was so fierce, I just kept quiet.

"Pick up that fallen chair, there's a good boy, and set it just to the right of the window," he directed me. "See how the light comes in?" He positioned me with my hands folded loosely in my lap. "Comfortable? Not too bad, *hmm*? Can you hold it like that for a while?"

Where had the raging monster gone? I was tense with waiting for it to reappear.

"Good lad," said Fitzgerald Cotton. "Now, where are my paints?"

"Behind you, there on the big easel," I snapped, not moving from my pose. "In that old wooden box." Was the man blind as well as crazy? He'd been using those paints just two minutes ago.

Fitzgerald Cotton shook his head. "Oh no, no, not *those* paints. Never those *special* paints—not for a portrait of *you*. Not with pigments more precious than gold!" He walked over and snatched up the box. It was a small wooden sort of trunk, about as big as a shoe box, but very dark and cracked. The wood was shiny, even though the box looked really old. It looked like somebody had polished the wood with great care.

"I keep this box under lock and key," Fitzgerald Cotton said, moving across the room to a big wardrobe in the corner. He had to step over his huge mess to get there, but when he did, he opened the cupboard and stashed the box deep inside. Then he locked the door and slipped a key into his bathrobe pocket. What a weirdo.

"Those paints are my special paints," Fitzgerald Cotton hissed at me. His eyes gleamed with excitement or something. An unpleasant smile lingered on his lips. "Those paints are called tempera. They're incredible. I use them only for my finest works. They're the sort of pigments every artist dreams of owning, and they are very, *very* rare." Fitzgerald Cotton shook a pink-smeared finger in front of my nose. "They must be used only for the most important paintings—because once they're gone, there's no replacing them. Do you follow?"

"Um—not really," I said, shifting slightly on the hard seat. I scanned the room, looking for any sign of the sketch. Everything was such a mess—the single piece of paper could have been stashed *anywhere*.

He set a small blank canvas on another easel and positioned it about eight feet away from me. Then he grabbed up a kidney-shaped palette with lots of messy dabs of paint everywhere. "These paints will do for the likes of you," he told me, shifting his chair so that he was behind the easel and I couldn't see much of him anymore. "They're good paints. Perfectly ordinary oil paints. Nothing special, but fine for a nice ordinary subject—like you." He peered at me from around the easel, eyes narrowed.

"I save my tempera pigments for my muse," he told me. "Those particular powders aren't just any old paints—though they are very, very old indeed. *Incredibly* old. How old do you think?" When I didn't answer, he barked at me, "How old?"

"Uh—like, five years?" I ventured.

"Hah! Try five *hundred* years!" Again Fitzgerald Cotton's face peered at me from around the canvas. "MORE THAN FIVE HUNDRED YEARS! Those pigments are my treasure. They're extraordinary."

He repositioned my hands, then stepped back to study me. "All right, hold it like that. And don't look so stupid. So *vacant*. You can't expect me to paint you, looking like a dullard. You need to think about something to engage your mind—and your expression."

"Can I talk while you paint?"

"Certainly, but don't move."

As soon as somebody tells me to keep still, I feel like twitching and jumping around and stuff. But I tried. I concentrated on my mission—finding the sketch. I moved only my eyes, looking around for it. But I could tell I'd never find it in all the mess. There must be another way.

"Um, do you do other kinds of art?" I asked hesitantly, mumbling a little so not to move my mouth much. "I mean, like sculpture or—you know. Sketches?"

"No sculpture, boy. Paint is my medium. The canvas is my kingdom—the brush is my sword! I sketch a few preliminary poses of my model in charcoal, but then I use oils or, in special cases, tempera. Both are complex mixtures, young man. They need to be—to catch the complexity of the people who sit for me."

"And what do you do with the charcoal sketches afterward?" I ventured. "Do you keep them? Like, um, in a special drawer somewhere?" I looked quickly around the studio.

"Hold still!" he shouted at me. His arm moved back and made a few stabbing motions at the canvas, but of course I couldn't see what was taking shape. "No," he said in a calmer voice. "I don't keep the sketches. Unless—unless they are special to me." He scowled at me over the top of the canvas. "Why do you ask?"

"No reason," I said hastily. We sat in silence for a few minutes, and I tried not to look over at the canvas that held the ghastly portrait of Mom.

He saw the direction of my look and nodded. "For my muse I use only the best paints. My special ones. Pure history in every brush stroke, my boy, in every color."

He paused and gave me that little unpleasant smile. "Sit still now, and I shall illuminate their history for your edification."

"Okay," I said. "Whatever." I watched him peering at me intently around the side of the easel. Then he started dabbing paint onto the canvas in broad strokes—and talking a mile a minute. I thought fleetingly of Homer and Chester out in the lemon grove making their tree fort. I thought of Betty and Elsie playing dolls on the porch. I wanted to be with them, not here. The tree fort sounded fun, but, hey—I'd even play with paper dolls. This guy was creepy.

"It was in Europe, see, after the war," Fitzgerald Cotton said. "I went to Italy to study painting. There's always something new to learn, and what better place to work than at the Academia, with all of Rome around me for inspiration? Besides, I had a special reason to go there. Centuries ago one of my ancestors made quite a name for himself as one of the Magi Painters. I'd always had a feeling in my bones that I must go there myself, back to the old sod. Back to the land of my forefathers. I visited all the museums to view the Old Masters—some of the most famous paintings in the world, my boy! I wanted to see the real thing, not poorly tinted photographs in art books."

He rubbed his hands together and leaned toward me. "While I was there at the Academia, I studied the techniques of one very special school of painters—the group who called themselves the Magi, the group my own ancestor had been part of. Can you imagine the honor?

And my excitement! This group painted together at the end of the fifteenth century, my boy, during the Renaissance. They were men from Rome and Venice and Padua, sought after by princes and kings, and their philosophy was that painting caught the essence of a subject, captured its very soul on canvas! I was amazed at the intricacy of their work—such delicacy! Such intensity! And what color! I would give anything, I thought, to be able to paint as they did. And then I met a professor of art at the university in Rome who was making it his life's work to track down samples of the actual paints used by painters of the past. The man had little pouches of powder—Michelangelo's blue and Uccello's greens! He had dabs of Botticelli's reds and Raphael's yellows and golds. Can you imagine my excitement, boy? I decided I must try to obtain some paints used by members of the Magi School. I hoped that with such paints I could capture the pure essence of my subject as they did theirs."

Capture, I thought. That was a very scary word.

Fitzgerald Cotton pushed his chair away from the easel. "Obtaining some of those old pigments became my quest," he continued, his voice deepening with the passion he felt about his subject. "At last I was rewarded—though I had to sell many of my finest paintings to come up with the money. Still, trading mere money for such an incredible link to past masters—maybe even to my own ancestor!—that was no hardship for me, boy. It was an honor!"

He strode over to the bookshelves that lined the wall by the door. "Look at these," he said, coming back to me, flipping through the pages of a large, heavy book. I broke my pose to lean forward and see what he was pointing at. He tapped the page. "Here they are," he said reverently. "Works of the Magi School."

The book was called *Renaissance Art,* and the pictures he pointed out to me were black-and-white photographs of paintings. The paintings were all of ordinary things—at least, I guessed they were ordinary in the fifteenth century—like cottages hunkered by the sea, and fields of sheep grazing, and grinning men wearing funny tall black hats and raising glasses to each other, and women carrying water from a well, and schoolboys sitting on a bench and holding slates on their laps, and little girls working at big spinning wheels. There were religious paintings of scenes from the Bible, like Adam and Eve in a huge garden. That one was shown in color, but the colors seemed sort of washed out.

Fitzgerald Cotton tapped the page. "I saw that one," he said. "Saw it in the flesh, so to speak. The colors are extraordinary—photography just can't do it justice. Maybe someday people will figure out how to print colors, but until then, this is what we get. Hand-tinted stuff." He snorted disdainfully. "Nothing like the real thing, let me tell you, boy."

Of course, in my time color photography had been figured out, but I couldn't tell him that. I just turned the page and looked at some portraits of rich-looking people in fancy clothes. These had all been tinted. One portrait especially stood out.

It showed a beautiful young woman. She sat on a

fancy padded bench in a sort of stone castle room with tapestries on the walls behind her. The detail in the painting was amazing—*exquisite,* to use one of Ms. Rose's spelling words. The lady looked familiar.

I got up to take the book out of Fitzgerald's hands, then sank down on the couch, staring at the picture of the lady in the book. There was something about her expression. She looked—*captured.*

I looked more closely at the page. The portrait had a caption under it. It said, FRANCESCA RIGOLETTI, 1479.

Rigoletti! That was Mom's last name!

I could feel my pulse in my temples. My whole head was pounding now. I closed my eyes, but even then I could still see the portrait in my head.

No wonder the woman in the portrait seemed familiar. The hair was darker, and she was younger—but she looked just like Mom.

∽ Chapter 9 ∽

An Evil Smile

The room was very quiet, but inside my head the pounding was deafening. *Find out, find out, find out,* thundered my heartbeat. Find out what the connection was between this long-ago woman and my mom. Find out because if I didn't, Mom would never, ever be safe. I don't know how I knew this, but the thought was there. *There is a connection, and Mom is in danger, and I have to figure it out.*

I could feel Fitzgerald Cotton watching me closely as I slowly turned the page.

In black-and-white or tinted with color, the photos of the old paintings seemed to glow; they were like Fitzgerald Cotton had described: luminous. Something about the way the artists painted light. Pretty cool, if you like paintings—which I wasn't sure I did anymore, to tell you the truth.

Fitzgerald Cotton sat down next to me on the couch. I moved away from him so that our arms weren't touching or anything.

He reached over and took the book. He flipped through some more pages and pointed out paintings done in the same style, bragging about the originals he had seen in Rome and Venice, and droning on about how amazing the true colors were. I just stared dully down at them, my mind searching for answers. Lots of people had the same last name, I reminded myself. Rigoletti might be a really common name in Italy, for all I knew. And lots of people look like other people. Maybe there were loads of people in Italy who looked sort of like Mom. . . .

Fitzgerald Cotton tapped his finger on one of the pages. "Look here," he ordered, and I did, trying to concentrate. More portraits, but this time they were all faces of men with beards and funny caps with feathers. "The Magi School artists," Fitzgerald Cotton said reverently. "They painted one another's portraits for posterity."

Again, one portrait stood out. But this time it wasn't because the guy looked familiar—not exactly. But there was . . . something.

"Who was this person?" I asked, pointing to the portrait of a wild-looking man, younger than the others, with especially unnerving eyes. They were piercing and narrowed and seemed to have a fire in the pupils. But it was the smile that really got me. A creepy, cold little quirk of the lips. A smile that held nothing happy or funny in it—only nastiness. And secrets.

I had a bad feeling about that guy.

Fitzgerald Cotton stroked the pages with one long finger. "Ah, yes, *that* man."

The studio door opened and Betty stepped in. We both looked up, startled out of the tension that had settled over us as we looked at the book. "*There* you are!" Betty said to me, sounding exasperated. "Didn't you hear the lunch bell?"

I shook my head. But I was glad to see Betty. It was as if some of the evil I felt in the studio was banished when she opened the door.

"Excuse me, Uncle Fitz. But Gramma has been looking for Connor." Betty came over to us and stood by the couch. "What are you two looking at?" She peered down at the book. "Who's that creepy fellow?"

Fitzgerald Cotton shifted on the couch next to me. "Sit down a moment, Betty, girl, and get an education. I was just telling Connor about an ancestor of mine. Yours, too, dear girl. This fellow was the black sheep of the Magi Painters. He was Lorenzo da Padova—some people say he was a madman if ever there was one. Murdered his own brothers, it was said at the time, so he might inherit his family's fortune uncontested. No one ever proved anything against him, but people knew, just the same. People tried to stay out of his way—and yet his paintings were the best of the bunch."

"How horrid!" Betty exclaimed. "How perfectly terrible to have somebody like that on our family tree!"

"Nonsense, dear child," said her uncle. "We should feel honored. He was a genius, and an artist of the highest caliber. True—some said an *evil* genius. Dabbled in poisons, some said. Others said black magic. However, you don't judge art by its creators, children. The work transcends everything. It's much more than the sum of its parts, do you understand me?"

Betty shook her head. "You mean that the paint and the canvas and the subject matter and even the artist himself all come together to form something great—and it doesn't matter what sort of person puts it all together? Like, even if the artist is really nasty, the painting can be beautiful?"

Fitzgerald Cotton beamed up at her. "Well said. That's exactly what I mean. The artist is the facilitator. Art happens *through* him. The painting is a thing separate from him, even though he painted it."

Sort of as if the painting becomes its own self, I guessed he was saying. Sort of like how you can really enjoy a film, even if you hear that the actors are total dorks in real life, or conceited or bad-tempered. The film can be winning awards and stuff, even if the actors are thrown in jail on drug charges or whatever. Art stands alone.

It sounded like a good slogan, but I didn't like the look of that da Padova guy. Not one bit.

"Well, I still wish he'd been a nice person," Betty said staunchly.

"Nice?" Fitzgerald Cotton laughed. "*Nice* is next to nothing. Anybody can be nice. But only a very special person could mix paints that would hold their colors so well over time. And could use those paints to express the essence of his genius so well." His eyes grew bright and feverish. "And now some of those same pigments the Magi Painters used to paint these paintings reside right here in my very own studio," Fitzgerald Cotton exulted. He closed the big book reverently and gave it a pat. "I own a piece of history. A piece of immortality. It's my way of making magic, of being one of the Magi. And with their pigments I try to make magic of my own. It was working beautifully for a while. I was inspired. Now—well, now it's all gone..."

He stood up and took the book over to the cluttered table. I could hear the shouts of Homer and Chester out in the backyard. "I suppose you both must go down to lunch now."

"Yes," I said. And you'd think I'd be running out of there like a prisoner set free. But instead I just stood there.

The big art book lay on the table. Fitzgerald Cotton's paintings were on canvases all over the room. The woman in the portrait in the book was named Francesca Rigoletti. The woman in the portrait on the big canvas was my mom. And her name was Pamela Rigoletti.

There had to be a connection—or why else was I here?

The dizziness I had fought off when I'd first landed here in the past swept over me now. Facts were swirling around in my head, fluttering like moths, impossible to pin down. Francesca Rigoletti looked like Pamela Rigoletti—my mom. Mom had been swept back here to this house, to this studio. Fitzgerald Cotton painted her using paints that once belonged to the Magi Painters....And now that he was painting her from memory, the paintings all turned out to be fearful portraits of a woman in pain.

How did all these pieces fit together? And what part could Lorenzo da Padova, Cotton's evil ancestor, have in this strange puzzle? My head ached with trying to make sense of it all, and I knew now that my quest in this time—my mission, if I chose to accept it—was no longer just to find that sketch and blow myself safely home again. Now I needed to find out what was going on with my mom.

And save her.

"May I borrow the big book, Uncle Fitzy?"

I looked at Betty, startled. She gave me a little smile and asked again. "Please? I think Connor and I would both like to look at the paintings by the Magi artists some more."

"I suppose." Fitzgerald Cotton sounded distracted. He moved back to stand in front of the portrait of Mom. "Just don't spill your soup on it."

"We will be very careful," Betty promised. "Now, aren't you coming down to lunch with us? Gramma said I was to tell you to come."

Her uncle shook his shaggy head. "You go. I must paint." And it was as if he were already off in another world. He opened the wardrobe and pulled out the old wooden box. He opened the box, and we watched as he started mixing colors. First he selected an egg from the bowl on the table in the center of the room, and broke it deftly, sliding the yolk into a cup and letting the runny white and the shell drop into the sink. He sifted in some of the colored powder—red—and added a drop of water from the tap. Furiously he stirred the mixture, then tested the shade on his palette, lost in his own weird world. "Trouble, trouble," he said mournfully. "Always just one trouble piling upon the next. And now no muse. The final blow." He spoke quietly, as if to himself, as if he'd forgotten we were there.

"Oh, heavens!" cried Betty, seeing Mom's portrait on the big easel for the first time. "That's awful! Why are you making Pammie look like that?"

"I'm not *trying* to, my girl," he replied grimly. "This is what comes out."

"You won't get the real Pammie back by painting her, Uncle Fitz," Betty said, watching him stroke colors onto the canvas. It was almost as if she'd read my mind. She shuddered. "And why you'd want to preserve her looking so hideous—like *that*—I can't imagine."

"But I *must* paint her!" he shouted suddenly, whirling on us. "Don't you see? I *must* paint her. I shall always paint her—to the end of my days. Even though the blasted paints don't work properly anymore! Could be the old pigments are breaking down with age, turning sour. I've heard it happens..." His voice trailed off, and he turned back to the canvas.

My mind started ticking. I struggled up off the couch, my gaze fixed on Fitzgerald Cotton as he painted frantically at his easel. I felt I was so close to understanding something—something important. Something vitally important to me, and to Mom.

But the glimmer faded. I thought I could hear Mom urging me to help, but her voice was only the merest whisper in my head.

"Come on," Betty said to me softly, lifting the heavy book off the table and holding it like a shield across her chest.

Reluctantly I stood up and left the crazy painter to his awful work. I followed Betty out of the studio, down the attic stairs, with Mom's anguished whisper wafting after me: *Come back, Connor. Come back.*

Back home? Or back up to the studio? Either way, it was time to make a plan.

∼ Chapter 10 ∼

Romantic Mr. Riley

*S*till in my daze I followed Betty out of the studio and down the stairs. She carried the big art book and stopped off to drop it on the dresser in her bedroom. "Gramma's got lunch waiting," she told me. "We can look at the book after. *If* you come clean with me."

That brought me out of the daze. "I don't know what you mean."

"You know. You know where Pammie went; I'm sure you do. I was sure from the second I met you. And you must know more—like why that lady in Uncle Fitz's art book looks so much like her." She stomped down the next flight of stairs ahead of me, and went out onto the porch, where Mrs. Cotton was serving our lunch.

The whole time we were eating tomato soup and cheese sandwiches, and drinking freshly made lemonade, Homer and Chester chattered about their fort. Elsie begged Joanna to take her to the toy store in town. Betty kept giving me mean looks. I kept thinking of how I had to get into that studio alone and search it. Find the sketch. *Make things happen.* I liked the unfamiliar sound of that. I wondered if I could ask Betty to help me. She seemed like the kind of girl who got things done, who didn't take no for an answer.

Fitzgerald Cotton never came down for his meals. He probably even slept up there, on the couch. So how was I ever going to get into the studio without him seeing me? Maybe he would creep down to use the bathroom— I mean, the guy had to pee sometime, didn't he? I could keep a sharp eye on him and sneak into the studio while he was downstairs.

Maybe he came down other times, too, like in the dead of night—to raid the refrigerator or something. Except there wasn't a refrigerator to raid—just something that *looked* like a fridge, called an icebox. It had shelves inside, and a big, deep sort of place at the bottom for a humongous chunk of ice. The ice kept things cool until it melted. Yesterday at dinnertime I'd seen Mrs. Cotton emptying a pan of water, and she explained to me that the iceman would deliver a new block of ice the next morning.

Sure enough, while we were eating lunch on the porch, a horse-and-cart came down the road. The cart was closed in at the back like a little truck, and the words painted on the side said:

MASON'S—WE BRING THE NORTH POLE
TO YOUR ICEBOX

"Look!" I called out in excitement. It was totally cool to have this big shaggy horse clopping right down the street and stopping at the Cottons' gate. It even took my mind off my worries and plans for the moment. But everyone just looked at me like *duh*. Like if a kid looked out at *my* street and said, "Look, a car!"

Then I felt a little sly smile twitch my mouth. "Hey, Betty!" I said to her. "Hey, look!"

"Hay is for horses," Betty replied primly.

"And there's the very horse, at your service." I laughed, pointing. "Right, Homeboy?"

Homer cracked up. He was all right, really. Elsie laughed and repeated what I'd said, over and over: "Hay is for horses—and here comes the very horse! Hay is for horses—and here comes the ice horse!"

Chester called out to the driver, "*Hey,* Mr. Riley, need some *hay* for your horse?"

And then the horse threw back its big shaggy head, shook its mane, and neighed loud and long. Even Betty had to giggle at that.

But she stopped giggling when Mr. Riley tipped his cap at us and jumped down from his seat high up on the wagon.

"Here comes trouble," she muttered.

"Who is he?" I whispered.

But Betty didn't answer—just crossed her eyes at me.

I watched this Mr. Riley guy. He went around to the back of the wagon to open the door. He dragged out a burlap sack with the gigantic block of ice inside. The ice was packed in straw. You could see bits sticking out all over the place.

Mr. Riley was about fifty, older than my dad but

built the same—like a football player. Big muscles from hefting around all that heavy ice. Looked like Mr. Riley didn't need to work out at a gym, because his work *was* the workout.

"What's the matter with him?" I asked the kids. "He looks all right."

"He's trying to woo Mama," Homer whispered to me. "And Betty hates him for it. I don't like him much, either."

"He's smarmy," added Elsie. "And he can't abide children. He doesn't like us."

"But he pretends to," muttered Betty. "To butter up Mama."

"The only good thing about him is his horse!" said Chester. "If he married Mama, we could ride Nellie every day." He ran to help Mr. Riley lug the ice up onto the porch.

"Mr. Riley doesn't really own Nellie," said Elsie. "She belongs to Mr. Mason, who owns the ice company. Mr. Riley is just one of his hired deliverymen. But Chester doesn't understand."

Betty frowned. "And he doesn't understand how it would be having Mr. Riley for our father. You can practically smell his dislike of us." She bit her lip.

"*Pee-yewww,*" said Elsie.

"Watch how he won't ever look at us," added Homer. "He just sort of *won't* see us. It's as if we're no more than ants to him. I bet if he and Mama got married, he'd try to ship us off to some boarding school or military academy before you could blink."

Mrs. Cotton was directing Mr. Riley into the kitchen with the block of ice. When he came out again, he accepted a glass of lemonade and stayed to chat with the grown-ups for a while. Homer was right—he didn't even look at us kids, and only barely glanced up and nodded when Mrs. Cotton introduced me to him as their special guest. He just sort of muttered hello to me, never once meeting my eye, but then turned a beaming smile on Joanna. Joanna seemed happy enough to see him, though, and Mrs. Cotton was chattering at him like he was the greatest guy in the world. Or maybe she was just glad to have ice.

At least he took time to sit and chat. I mean, at home in my own time, we never see the people who help us out or make deliveries or come to repair things. They come and do their jobs while we're at work and school...and it's probably against their union policy to accept any food or drink. Mrs. White just lets them in and out, and they leave their bill on the kitchen counter.

Mr. Riley sat in one of the rocking chairs. He hitched his chair closer to Joanna's and talked mostly to her. "Lovely day, isn't it? Warm as summertime. Maybe you'd like to take a walk with me one evenin' this week, just around the town, stop for coffee at Maxwell's Café or perhaps the Walnut Inn?"

Joanna smiled at him. "Thank you," she said. "Either would be very nice."

Betty glowered at them both. Homer looked like he might start hissing and booing the way they did at old-time plays when the villain came onstage.

Mrs. Cotton looked up at all of us standing along the

porch railing. "You children run off now and play," she said.

"Don't they go to school?" Mr. Riley asked her, frowning in our general direction. He could have asked *us* since we were practically right there in front of his nose. I could tell Betty and Homer didn't like being ignored. And they clearly had no intention of running off to play.

"It's Easter week," Joanna reminded him.

"Ah yes." He drank his lemonade and rocked back and forth. "When I was a lad, the swimming hole was the place to be during Easter week. All my pals would meet there. We had races; we had games. We would climb the nearest tree and drop down into the water from the highest branches—"

"Hey!" interrupted Chester. "Let's go to the swimming hole!"

Mr. Riley winked at Joanna, and I knew he'd been hoping to get us interested so we'd run off and swim and leave him in peace with Joanna. It looked like Betty had figured that out, too, because she snapped, "It will be freezing at the swimming hole! And Mr. Riley knows it."

"Betty," chided her mother, "mind your manners."

Homer's glowering look had softened at Mr. Riley's mention of the swimming hole, and now both Chester and Elsie were all over their mother.

"Hooray!" they cried. "We love the swimming hole! May we go?"

"Betty's right about its still being too cold now, I think," Joanna replied.

Mr. Riley inched his chair a bit closer to hers. "Ah,

well, kids are hearty, aren't they? Now, my dear Joanna—ah, Mrs. Cotton—" He leaned closer, trying for a little privacy. "How about we set a date to take in a moving picture over at the cinedrome? I hear *Rin-Tin-Tin* is all the rage."

"Why, yes, Mr. Riley," said Joanna, with her sweet smile. "I would enjoy accompanying you to a moving picture. Thank you very kindly."

"It will be an honor," said Mr. Riley.

"I want to see *Rin-Tin-Tin,* too," Elsie announced, but Mr. Riley ignored her. He drained his lemonade glass.

"That hit the spot," he said, standing up and bowing slightly, first to Mrs. Cotton and then to Joanna. "Thank you kindly, Mrs. Cotton and Mrs. Cotton, but I'll need to be on my way again. Nellie's waiting—and so is the ice. The water may still be too cold for swimming, but this *is* a hot spell we're having, and no mistake about it. I've had to fill dozens of orders for extra ice just since Monday, when the temperature shot up."

"We'll see you again next week, Mr. Riley," said Mrs. Cotton. "If not before." She slanted a meaningful glance over at her daughter-in-law.

"Might have to be before then, ma'am, if this heat holds," Mr. Riley said, walking down the steps. "Last lady I delivered to said her block of ice lasted only three days. She came down this morning and found a gigantic puddle of water in the kitchen. Thought she'd sprung a leak somewhere—but it was only the ice block."

"I'll telephone you if we need another order," Joanna said.

"I'll be telephoning *you* this evening, to fix a date for *Rin-Tin-Tin,*" he reminded her. "And perhaps dinner beforehand? The Walnut Inn does a lovely meal—nicer, really, than Maxwell's."

Next to me Betty was gritting her teeth. "The Walnut Inn's a fancy place with candlelight and harp music," she muttered.

"He's getting goopy," whispered Homer. "What're we going to do?"

I watched thoughtfully as Mr. Riley jumped back up onto the high seat of his wagon and whistled to Nellie. As they set off down the street, he tipped his hat to Joanna and Mrs. Cotton. The ladies waved back at him.

"We have to save Mama," whispered Elsie.

"We have to save ourselves," replied Betty. "I don't want to go away to boarding school."

"We'll make a plan," agreed Homer. "Wanna help us save Mama, Connor?"

But I was barely listening to them. I was thinking about ice blocks melting into big puddles. Mr. Riley might not have looked at me for even two seconds, but he had just given me a wonderful idea—an idea I was rapidly forming into a plan for how to get into the studio and maybe save my *own* mama.

I wanted to look at that art book again, but it was up in Betty's bedroom, and she and Joanna had gone in there after lunch and closed the door. Joanna was fitting Betty for a new dress she'd been sewing on the black iron sewing machine in the dining room. So I spent the next hour of that hot day playing Snakes and Ladders with the other kids, on the shady porch. The game sort of grows on you. It helped that I kept winning. But then I got restless. It felt wrong to be sitting around when I needed to find out how Fitzgerald Cotton was capturing my mom. Not to mention that I still hadn't found any trace of the sketch that had brought me here. My mind was ticking along as I moved my piece around the game board. I was working on my plan.

If my plan worked I'd get into the studio that very night—and maybe be on my way home to Mom. But in the meantime it wouldn't hurt to see something of 1926 besides this porch and this game board.

"Hey, guys," I said to the kids. "How about that swimming hole?"

"Hay is for—oh, never mind." Betty stepped out onto the porch. "Mama's finished with me at last. Let's go upstairs." She looked at me. "And educate ourselves about art."

"I like the idea of the swimming hole," said Homer, "better than art!"

"You go ahead," Betty told him. "But Connor and I have some unfinished business." She gave me a look, eyebrows raised. "We need to have a little talk."

We do? I thought uneasily. She was a pain, and I knew she was going to try to get me to tell her my whole life story—the true one. I wasn't ready for that. I did want to look at that art book—but I wanted to do it alone. "I vote we go swimming," I said, raising my eyebrows right back at Betty.

"But Mama says it's too cold," said Elsie.

"We don't have to swim if we don't want to," I pressed. "I just want to see it. It sounds cool."

Homer looked puzzled. "I don't see how it can *sound* cool," he said. "It might turn out to *be* cold, but how can it *sound* that way?"

"Forget about it, Homeboy," I said, standing up. "Come on."

Homer and I walked down the steps, and of course Chester and Elsie ran after us. After a minute, before we'd even reached the sidewalk, Betty joined us. "All right," she said. "We can talk about how to foil Mr. Riley."

"He didn't seem that bad," I said mildly, mostly to see her reaction.

"He is bad!" she snapped. "He wants to marry Mama! But I'm sure Mama doesn't love him. She just thinks that we need a father. Well, I say we don't—especially not a father who won't give us the time of day."

"If she married anybody, it really should be Uncle Fitzy," said Elsie. "That's the one I think she really loves. I mean, after Daddy, of course."

"He's too grumpy," said Chester.

"Yes, but married to Mama, he wouldn't be," said Homer loyally.

We passed four other houses, then reached the corner of Lemon Street—the corner where, in my time, the school bus picked me up every morning. We crossed East Main—the road Homer said led into the town—and headed down a dirt path off to the right. I was looking around for street signs, trying to orient myself. *Our* house was on Lemon Street, and Lemon Street bisected East Main, but East Main in *my* time was just a long stretch in a housing development, with streets named after fruits branching off it, each ending in a cul-de-sac. Each street had about twenty big houses on it, not all exactly alike, but very similar, built by the same developer. I looked around me now for Orange Street and Blueberry Drive and Almond Lane, but they weren't anywhere. The streets were quiet—hardly any traffic at all. No hum in the distance from the freeway, either.

Since this was my neighborhood, you'd think I'd recognize something. But so far I hadn't, except for Mount Diablo. Where Doug's house ought to be, there were just zillions of trees. In fact, there were big groves of lemon trees between all the houses on Lemon Street—and there were only about four or five houses, anyway, not the twenty or so that are crammed onto the street in my time. The houses on Lemon Street in 1926 all had big porches like the Cottons'. The street was paved, but then turned to this dirt track leading out of the lemon grove down to a stream.

Stream? Doug and I would have killed for a stream so close to home. Maybe if there were a stream, it would be worth going out after school to play. But I remembered learning in school how lots of the streams in the Bay Area had been built right over with streets and sidewalks. The streams were still there, running through the hills, down to the bay, but nobody ever saw them.

Seemed a stupid thing to do to a stream, I thought, as we followed this burbling one along till it widened out into a pool. The swimming hole.

"Kids made this swimming hole years and years ago," Homer told me proudly. "Kids dammed it up and made this pool."

"They worked like beavers!" said Chester. "Look how they used mud and sandbags to build the walls."

"Beavers don't use sandbags," snorted Betty. "Or rocks, either."

"Well, they would if they could," Chester retorted. He stripped off his clothes right there in front of everybody, right down to his underpants, walked over to the edge of the pool, and dipped his foot in. "Freezing!" he said. "Mama was right!"

"Our daddy and Uncle Fitzy swam here when they were boys," Elsie told me. "Uncle Fitzy taught Daddy to swim."

The swimming hole was about half as big as the pool in Doug's backyard, and maybe just about as deep. The water wasn't turquoise and bubbly, cleaned weekly by the Tid-ee-Pool maintenance company. The water was clear enough, though, that you could see down through it to the muddy bottom and along the rock and sand-bagged sides covered with ferns and water plants. It was unsupervised, unchlorinated, maybe unsafe—and it looked great to me. I stripped off my clothes, too, right down to my *Star Wars* underpants—and jumped in.

Homer shed his shirt but not his trousers, then joined us, screeching at the top of his lungs. After a few minutes so did both girls, though they kept their dresses on, and the full skirts floated around them like big jellyfish. We swam and splashed and ducked each other, shrieking like maniacs the whole time because the water really was so cold it made your bones ache.

I wished I'd brought my camera—or camcorder. *Fitzy should paint* this *instead of Mom,* I thought. *Capture* it *forever.*

The kids started talking about how to stop their mom from dating Mr. Riley. "We have to sabotage their date to the cinedrome," said Betty. "It's obvious. A romantic dinner at the Walnut Inn will ruin everything. He could propose to her there, and then what?"

"Boarding school, here we come," said Homer.

"We can't let them eat there," agreed Chester.

"Maybe we should just kill him," Elsie suggested casually. "Like, with poison."

"Elsie!" The others looked shocked. They sent splashes of cold water into her face.

"You don't just go around killing people who are in your way," Betty chided her. "Not even Mr. Riley. We have to be more subtle than that."

"Yeah," I agreed. "And prison would be a lot worse than boarding school, probably."

"I was just *joking,*" Elsie told us, rolling her eyes and shaking the water out of her hair. "But nobody else is thinking of anything!"

"I know—why don't we poison *ourselves*?" Chester suggested. "Then Mama will have to stay home to take care of us."

"Oh, *right,*" said Homer sarcastically. He sent a huge wave of freezing water over his brother's head.

But Betty was grinning. She reached out and ducked Homer. When he came up, sputtering, she said, "No, wait— Chester's brilliant. That's exactly what we'll do. Oh, not *really,*" she said when Homer opened his mouth to protest. "But we'll all get really ill—come down with something *dire*—just before she's going to leave with Mr. Riley."

I laughed at them, shaking my head. "Don't forget, your grandparents will be there, and your uncle," I reminded them. After all, Crystal and I have stayed home sick plenty of times with Ashleigh or Mrs. White—or once even with Gregorio, the old gardener who didn't speak two words of English—because our parents had to work or had tickets for the opera or something.

Betty, Homer, Elsie, and Chester all just stood gaping at me. "Well, *of course* Mama wouldn't go out if we were sick!" Elsie said. "What kind of mother would do *that*?"

I ducked under the water and swam to the other side of the pond. *Never mind.*

Finally we traipsed back home. We were wet and muddy. Mrs. Cotton exclaimed that we'd all probably caught our deaths, but Joanna, who was sitting with her on the porch mending clothes with a dreamy sort of expression on her face, just sent us around to the back door to sluice off with buckets of fresh water before coming into the house. I thought maybe she was dreaming about her dates with Mr. Riley, and you could tell

Betty was thinking the same thing. She stomped upstairs to change her clothes like each step had a nasty bug on it named Mr. Riley. *Stomp, squash! Stomp, squish!*

Homer gave me a pair of knee-length pants—*britches,* he called them—that were too big for him. They were hand-me-downs from some neighbor, and he was supposed to grow into them sooner or later. A soft white cotton shirt that buttoned up the front came from the same guy, and so did the weird kneesocks that fit under the buttoned cuffs of the pants. Now I looked like Homer, without the glasses, but at least I was dry.

"You'll have to keep your own shoes, I'm afraid," Homer said regretfully.

"That's fine," I told him, relieved, though they sure looked silly with black-and-red diamond-patterned knee-socks. "Thanks a lot."

❧

Meet me in my room to look at the book," Betty hissed when I came out of the boys' bedroom in my new "duds"—but just then Joanna called the girls to help with the mending. Betty stamped her feet and pouted, and I knew she was frustrated at being thwarted again, but there was nothing she could do about it. Crystal would have point-blank refused to attempt mending of any sort, but Betty was different that way. She fussed and fumed, but she obeyed her mother.

I wanted to sneak into the girls' room and get the art book to look at on my own, but Joanna set us boys to weeding in the backyard. At home I might have refused—not that I'd ever been told to weed anything, since we had old Gregorio. But here I didn't dare make a fuss. So I went out with them, and I learned how to tell a weed from a flower after Chester shrieked at me a couple times for pulling out the jasmine plants.

"So what sort of sickness are you going to come down with?" I asked Chester, trying to distract him from watching every weed I pulled. He was kneeling next to me on the grass, and he sat back on his heels to give my question serious consideration.

"Maybe scarlet fever," he said musingly. "I could paint a sort of rash on my belly and cheeks with red watercolors. I'm pretty good at painting, you know. Runs in the family."

"No, Chess, not scarlet fever," Homer objected from over by the geraniums. "Nothing too serious or Mama will call for the doctor. The doctor would know your rash was only paint in two seconds, and then we'd all be in really hot water."

I tugged at a prickly weed as they discussed the problem. They'd already had measles and chicken pox and mumps, so they couldn't come down with those again. And Betty had scarlet fever when she was a baby. Then they started talking about some little cousin of theirs who had died of some sickness called diphtheria.

I hadn't had any of those sicknesses, of course, because I'd been vaccinated against them. But maybe in 1926 there weren't any such things as immunizations.

They hadn't decided on a sickness by the time Joanna called us in for dinner. First, she showed me how to set the table. The girls came in from the porch with their pile of mended clothing, neatly folded. Then we all sat down together, just like the night before, and prayed that God would bless our meal. Then we ate a delicious pie with chunks of chicken and vegetables and gravy inside a flaky crust. We told about the high points of our day.

I talked about sitting for my portrait—but I didn't give any details of the scene up in the studio. Homer and Chester told about the tree fort. Elsie held up a little pink striped dress she had made for one of her dolls. Betty asked her grandpa about their ancestor Lorenzo da Padova.

"Ah, yes," the old man said meditatively. "That would be on your gramma's side—her mother's father was born in Italy and emigrated to America, isn't that right, dear? Or your grandmother's father? Something like that."

"I don't really recall," said Mrs. Cotton. "But I do remember hearing that there was a well-known painter very long ago on some distant branch of our family tree. Ask your uncle Fitz about him, why don't you, Betty? He'll know much more than I do. He reveres all those old Italian fellows!"

"But some people thought Lorenzo was evil," pressed Betty. "Do you think he was?"

"Evil," mused Mr. Cotton. "That's a pretty heavy label to attach to anyone, seems to me. I don't know whether I believe in evil, dear child. Though some folks are *misguided,* that's for certain!"

"I think you're too kind, dear," said Mrs. Cotton. "*I*

believe in evil," she told us. "It's the absence of good, that's what it is. It's war and hatred and immorality— and I'm sure all our ancestors had as much of that to guard against long ago as we do now. The important thing is to keep trying to improve ourselves. Not to let evil get the upper hand." She passed the big dish of pie around the table again. "Now come along, all of you. It would be the very *worst* evil to waste a single bite of this lovely pie Joanna has made us!"

After dinner, while the girls cleared the table, Joanna glanced over at me. "Connor, dear? How about choosing a puzzle? We finished one just last week."

"It was a killer, that one was," said Mrs. Cotton, stacking up the dinner plates for Betty to carry to the kitchen. "Vicious amounts of sea and sky—all blue. Pick one with no blue, Connor."

I just sat there for a moment, uncertain what to do. I'd been planning to get to that art book at last, or at least to go off by myself somewhere and think about my plan for later that night. But Joanna was beckoning me over to the china closet. She tugged open the bottom door. There were stacks of puzzles inside on the shelves. "How about this one? The Presidential Garden." Joanna put the box on the table, and I saw it was a puzzle of a formal flower garden in front of the White House. Lots of flowers and trees and stuff, all in pinks and reds and yellows. Not a lot of blue. I was about to say I'd been to Washington, D.C., with my family two summers ago and had toured the White House . . . but then I realized I didn't know who the president was in 1926, and I didn't even know if they let people have tours in this time.

I did know that people in this time didn't slope off on their own to watch TV or read or anything after a meal the way we did at home. They sat around together some more, talking and—so it seemed—doing jigsaw puzzles. "Looks good to me" was all I said. We went out onto the porch, where the others were gathered, and showed them the box.

Mrs. Cotton nodded. "That'll do nicely. That puzzle was a gift to Fitz when he was a boy. Only way we could get him to stop painting was to buy him puzzles! And even then he'd come down only for a while...I think he's lived most of his life up in that studio of his." She pursed her lips and cast a glance at the ceiling as if she could see through to the attic, where Fitz was *still* hanging out. I wondered if he *ever* came downstairs.

Believe it or not, I nearly forgot about Fitzgerald Cotton and his art book once I started doing the puzzle. It was a hard one, and I planned to work on it only for a few minutes, just to make Mrs. Cotton and Joanna happy. But then it hooked me. Homer and Chester joined me, and so did Betty and Elsie when they had finished washing the dishes. We sat there all cozy, fitting the little pieces together and cheering when we finished a whole tree or flower bed. Aside from our cheering and the rustle of Mr. Cotton's newspaper, the porch was quiet. It really got to me—the near silence. The whole house was so quiet. No TV, no music, no phone. It was all very peaceful—almost as peaceful as the presidential garden looked in the puzzle taking shape under our hands.

We stayed out there until the dark deepened around us and Joanna announced it was time for bed. We said good night and went upstairs. I lay there in my narrow camp bed, hoping that Homer and Chess would drift off quickly. I could hear Elsie chattering to Betty in the other room, and Joanna's voice telling them to hush now and sleep. I wondered how long it would take before the adults came up to bed. There would be no late-night movie keeping them up; and there would be no Internet chat groups. So maybe it wouldn't take long.

I awoke with a start—furious at myself for having drifted off—and the house was dark and silent. No hall light shone outside the bedroom door. There was no murmur of voices from downstairs. I peered over at the other beds. Homer and Chester were just dark humps in the shadows. I pushed back my sheets and slid out of bed.

Now was my chance. *Hang in there, Mom.* Time for plan *A*.

∽ Chapter 11 ∽

A Life of Crime

O ut into the hallway, down the creaky stairs. I
hugged the wall the way spies do on TV. But
this was a real-life adventure, and I was the star.

Into the front hallway. Through the dining room.
Into the kitchen.

The night was warm and still. A slight breeze stirred
the white net curtains at the open window over the sink.
A sliver of moonlight lay across the kitchen table. There
was the icebox, over in the corner. I unlatched the icebox
door and swung it open. No little light came on inside
the way it does in our fridge at home, but I could make
out in the moonlight that the block of ice was still there
in the bottom tray.

The night was warm, but not warm enough to melt
the ice and flood the kitchen the way Mr. Riley had
described. *No problemo.* My plan was about appear-
ances—not reality.

I started opening cupboards, searching until I found
a large iron pot. It took two hands to lift it up to the

sink. Then I ran hot water into it, hoping the pipes wouldn't clank and wake anybody upstairs. It was really hard to lift the full pot out of the sink. Some water splashed out onto the floor—but that didn't matter. In another second there'd be a whole lot more.

I took a few steps with the heavy pot and then lowered it carefully to the floor in front of the icebox. I used a soup ladle to pour the hot water onto the block of ice. But it didn't melt as I thought it would. So I tipped the whole pot onto the ice.

Water gushed onto the floor, pooling under the icebox and running around the legs of the chairs at the kitchen table. I jumped back so I wouldn't get splashed. Was that how much water one of those giant blocks of ice would make? I wasn't sure. So I filled the pot once more and tipped it. If a person saw *this,* he would just throw a towel down over it. I mean, it wasn't exactly a flood or anything.

I hesitated, then filled the pot again. Another and another—I was on autopilot or something—until I suddenly noticed that the whole kitchen was swimming in about an inch of water. And still that huge block of ice wasn't melted.

But it really was a flood now—definitely more water than the ice block could have held. I grabbed a dish towel off the rail by the sink, and looked at it helplessly. I heard Crystal's scornful voice in my head: *You always go too far, Connor!*

It was true this time, anyway. One towel would never work to sop up this mess. And the water was trickling across the kitchen linoleum, under the kitchen door, and into the dining room! I thought of the shiny wooden floor in there, and the pretty patterned rug, and what Mrs. Cotton would say if she knew what I had done. I winced and raced for the stairs. Then I stopped and made myself wade back through the kitchen—lifting the too-long legs of my pajamas (well, Mr. Cotton's pajamas) to keep them out of the water—and dried the pot I'd used and put it carefully away in the cupboard.

Finally, heart pounding, I thumped up the stairs, and up the next flight to the attic. I paused outside of Fitzgerald Cotton's studio. There was a faint light showing under the door.

I knocked.

There was no answer. I knocked again and tried the doorknob. It turned and the door swung open, and there was Fitzgerald Cotton, in moonlight, jerking out of sleep on the battered couch in the back of the room.

"What the devil—" he said in a fuzzy, sleep-filled voice. "Go away, boy—it's not time for painting. A man's got to sleep sometime!"

"Sorry," I said, panting from running up the stairs. "I didn't know who to tell—but then I saw your light was on. It's—there's a flood downstairs! I went down because I was really hungry . . . Thought I could get myself a piece of bread. And then I saw this huge flood in the kitchen! I think it's the icebox—the ice must have melted in this heat, just the way Mr. Riley said it did!"

Fitzgerald Cotton sat up and rubbed his face. "A flood?"

"Yes! Hurry! It could be running out of the kitchen and into the other rooms!"

Fitzgerald Cotton stood up and headed for the door. "Grab some towels out of the bathroom, boy, and help me mop it up," he ordered. "And keep quiet—there's no need to wake my parents."

I had to start down after him or he'd suspect something. I stopped at the bathroom as he continued on down the stairs. Then I grabbed a few towels, tossed them down the stairs after him, and turned and ran back up to the attic studio.

I might have only seconds to search for the lost sketch. Where to start? I looked wildly around the studio. The big portrait of Mom—*trapped*—was covered, and I was thankful. But then I saw another painting of Mom on the small easel, and my heart thudded hard as I walked over to it. This time she was sitting on a couch—pressed back against the cushions—her hands outstretched as if to ward off an attacker. An attacker—or an artist? A large book rested open on her lap. In one out-flung hand she clutched a single rose. Her eyes were wide with desperation.

Oh, Mom!

I stared harder as I realized that I recognized that couch, those cushions, even the big book and the rose. It was our living room. It was Mom as I had seen her myself, frozen. Posing. Locked in time.

I drew in a thick breath, shocked at this proof that Fitzgerald Cotton was not painting my mom from memory as he claimed, but actually *seeing* her. Somehow.

I reached out fearfully and touched one finger to the canvas. Red paint burned my fingertip like a bee sting. I gasped and rubbed my finger furiously against my nightshirt. How could paint cause such pain? The paint was wet, and that meant it had been applied recently. But how in the world could Fitzgerald Cotton be seeing my mom in the future, and painting her in our own house, which hadn't even been built yet? None of this made sense—but one thing was certain: Fitzgerald Cotton was using his special ancient paints. The colors before me were incredible, just as he had described. The paintings of Mom seemed to pulse—as if there were some life force captured there. And my fingertip still stung.

I sped around the room, opening every cupboard, checking every shelf as I looked for clues to how he could control my mom from so distant a time. I felt underneath the couch cushions, looked behind the couch—nothing. The big wardrobe was locked. I pulled extra hard before moving on to search other places.

Then I found half a dozen canvases leaning against the wall, covered by the long curtains. I turned the paintings around, one by one, and I felt like someone had punched me in the gut. There, in every one of them, was Mom, trapped and frightened. There she was in our living room again, this time curled up with a cup of tea in her hand, lifted as if to drink. But she could not drink; she was frozen. A piece of pound cake lay on a plate on the table at her side. I had eaten some of that cake. I had come into the room and interrupted this pose!

I felt dizzy trying to understand. There was Mom in

another painting, standing in our ultramodern, state-of-the-art kitchen with one hand holding a knife steady over a tomato. Her eyes were great pools of terror, and beads of blood seeped out along her hairline—no, not blood, I remembered, but paint.

There she was in the family room, with a pile of soft green knitting on her lap, her neck muscles bulging with the strain of her fear. In every single picture her face was creased into an agonized grimace.

"Mom," I whispered desperately, letting the curtain fall back to hide the canvases. I felt sick to my stomach.

The locked wardrobe mocked me. I was certain there were answers in there.

Then I heard footsteps creaking up the stairs. Fitzgerald Cotton was coming back! I would never be able to figure this out tonight.

I'm so sorry, Mom.

I quickly stepped out of the room and started down the stairs, meeting Fitzgerald Cotton coming up. "D—did you stop the flood?" I stammered.

"There was no flood, boy."

"No flood? But I saw all that water—"

"Ice still frozen solid."

"But I saw—"

"Lots of water on the floor, though. Way, way too much to have come from any ice block. The very devil to mop up. Funny thing." His eyes were narrow in the faint light, peering at me. "Wonder how it got there..."

My heart was thudding hard, and I wanted to pass him but didn't quite dare.

He reached out one hand and pressed my shoulder. "Wonder where it came from, boy?"

"I don't know," I told him firmly. "Must be the pipes are leaking."

"*Hmm,*" he said. "*Hmmm.* So, now, what about that bread you wanted?"

"I'm not hungry anymore," I whispered. "Guess I'll just go on back to bed." I sidled past him. He smelled of paint, and something else. Rotten egg?

I felt him staring after me as I hurried down the hall to the room I shared with Homer and Chess, but I didn't look back. My fingertip burned in the darkness.

I opened the boys' bedroom door and slipped inside, then gasped—*a ghost!*

But, of course, it wasn't a ghost. Just Betty, standing in front of me in her long white nightgown, her finger raised to her lips in warning. "*Shhh!*" she hissed.

I ignored her and slid into bed, pulling the sheet up to my chin. "What do you want?" I whispered.

"What were you doing?" she hissed back at me. "Where were you?"

"Nothing. Nowhere," I said stupidly.

"*Shhh.* Keep your voice down." She stood over me. The sliver of moonlight through the window threw her shadow up high on the wall so it looked like a threatening monster. I was surrounded by them tonight.

"*Who are you?*" Betty pressed, keeping her voice very low. Her eyes were dark pools in the moonlight. "I don't believe you're an orphan at all. I think you've come here under false pretenses. I think you're an *impostor!*"

She leaned over me, her voice low and controlled, but shaking—with fury, I supposed.

"What is it you want from us?" she demanded. "Is it *money*? Are you out to swindle my grandparents? Or what? Are you a robber?"

"No!" I whispered back. "Of course I'm not!"

"There's something very strange about you," she continued. "And I don't like it. It—it's scaring me." She took a deep breath, and I thought I heard the catch of tears behind it.

She was *scared* of me? Brave Betty, you had to hand it to her. She thought I might be a danger to her family, and she was going to try to protect them.

I sat up in the narrow bed. "Listen, Betty," I whispered. "It's all right. I'm not any danger to you or your family. I promise."

"Did Pammie send you?" she demanded. "I *know* you know her—I can tell."

"How can you tell?" I asked. "I mean—what do you *mean,* you think I *know* her?"

But it was too late. I'd given myself away.

"I know you know her," Betty said. And this time she wasn't even bothering to keep her voice low. "You must be related to her. You look exactly like her, same face and everything."

"That's what my dad always says," I muttered. I was making mistakes left and right. But the burden of my story was getting too heavy. And those canvases up in the studio had really rattled me.

"So your father knows Pammie, too," Betty said

softly. She lowered herself to sit on the edge of my bed. It was so narrow, I thought her weight might tip us both over onto the floor. But it didn't. "Tell me about your father," she coaxed. "And about Pammie. And who you really are. And everything."

"There's nothing to tell. Absolutely nothing." I'd already had one narrow escape tonight, I told myself. Now it was time to manage another—because if I told Betty the truth, she'd never believe me. And she'd get really mad—like Crystal does if she thinks you're lying to her—and make a huge fuss about how I was an impostor and everything, and the Cottons would throw me out. I couldn't let that happen—not when I was so close to figuring out Fitzgerald Cotton's hold on my mom.

She didn't look angry, though, just sad. In the moonlight I could see her bewildered face. "You know, when someone lives with you for a year, you kind of get attached," she said softly. "I *liked* Pammie, and so it's really hard having you here. I believe you know what's happened to her. I'm sure you do! I just can't understand why you won't tell us—"

"I can't," I muttered.

"Tell us if she's happy, wherever she is now. And why it has to be such a secret. And—if she misses us." She sounded nearly in tears.

Did Mom miss this family? Not Fitzgerald, surely, but Betty and Homer and Joanna and the others? She was certainly trying hard to re-create their way of life back in our own time....

I didn't want Betty crying. I cleared my throat. "I

know I look like Pammie," I said carefully. "But I don't know much else. I think—I think I must have amnesia."

"*What?*" she yelped.

"*Shhh!*" I said quickly, glancing over at Homer's and Chester's beds. "Yeah, amnesia. That's what I said, and it's what I meant. Maybe I was in an accident or something, but who knows? All I know is, I found myself wandering around Shady Grove, lost, not knowing what was going on or who I was. Maybe I'll remember who I really am in the morning. After a good sleep."

She stood up, leaned over me, hands on hips. Her shadow reared up like an avenging angel. "Nice try," she snapped, and now she did sound furious, "whoever-you-are. *Amnesia!* Can't you come up with anything better?"

It was exactly what I was thinking myself. *You can do better than this. Time for plan* B. But not tonight. "Tomorrow," I whispered. Then I turned on my side and burrowed my head into the pillow, and I didn't open my eyes again until morning, not even when I heard—finally—the click of the door as Betty left the room.

✌ Chapter 12 ✍

The Skylight

In dreams I saw Mom's anguished face. In dreams I saw the horrible canvases with her portraits falling through space like starships out of control, spiraling down and down and down through time. In my dreams I must have been tossing and turning, because I woke up with a thunk—fallen from my camp bed onto the floor, wrapped like a mummy in my sheet.

My first thoughts were of getting back into that studio. But there was no chance—not before breakfast. Old Mrs. Cotton stood in the bedroom door. "Connor? My goodness, what are you doing down there?" Without waiting for my reply, she crossed the room and snapped open the curtains. "It's a lovely sunny day, and time's a-wastin'. The other children will be gobbling your food if you don't hurry down."

My second thoughts were of Betty and how she'd be waiting for me. "Yes, ma'am. I'll hurry," I said faintly. As soon as Mrs. Cotton left the room, I unwound myself from the sheet and went into the bathroom. I splashed cold water on my face and caught a deep breath of fresh morning air from the open window. Had my mom stood at this same sink, in front of this same mirror, looking at her new 1926 haircut before she had hurried down for breakfast with this same family?

I'm trying, Mom, I told her silently.

Again, an amazing feast was waiting down in the dining room, with bacon and eggs and toast and home-made jam. Mr. Cotton was already at the table, halfway through a big plate of food. The kids were all harassing Joanna because she was dressed up and ready to go out somewhere. My eyes met Betty's briefly, then we both looked away. But I'd seen her determined expression, and I realized she would not let me off easily next time we had a chance to talk alone.

"Mama's got a fella. Mama's got a fella!" chanted Elsie. Her mother laughed and went into the kitchen to help Mrs. Cotton bring out the rest of the breakfast food. Mr. Cotton patted his lips with his cloth napkin, then laid it down next to his newspaper. He said good-bye to everyone. Then he set off for work.

"Mr. Riley telephoned," Betty told me darkly when I sat down next to her. "Somehow he got some time off from his ice deliveries today—and he's taking Mama to lunch at the Walnut Inn." She didn't say a word about our conversation the night before. I wondered if maybe she *was* going to let me off the hook.

"Time for plan *A*," Homer whispered to me. "Are you with us?"

I nodded, but I was thinking about my own plan *B* instead. "What sickness?"

"A horrible rash," he said gleefully, passing me the platter of bacon. "We're going to have to think up a way to turn ourselves red. Elsie had a good idea—to go pick the early blackberries... Most of them are still green and hard, but some are red—and if we mash them up, we can make a kind of red paste, like a stain to turn our faces and bodies red..."

"The problem with that plan," Betty said, "is that the blackberry bushes are out by the swimming hole. We'd have to get there, find enough red ones, mash them up, turn ourselves red, and hurry back—and Mama's already dressed and ready to go. She'll be gone before we get back."

"We could run fast," suggested Chester.

"You guys are missing something," I said, lowering my voice as Mrs. Cotton and Joanna came over to the table with more toast and a pitcher of milk.

"Such as?" asked Betty, one eyebrow raised the way I always wished I could raise mine. But mine only go up and down together.

"Such as you have an uncle who's an artist, with a big studio and tons of supplies. Why go all the way to the swimming hole to mash up berries and stuff, when there's all the paint in the world right upstairs?" *Just don't use the old stuff,* I thought to myself. My finger still stung and a small blister had formed at the tip.

The four kids just looked at me. "Go in Uncle Fitzy's studio?" Elsie said. "Are you crazy?"

"It's simple," I said easily. "Just go when he's in the bathroom or something."

"He takes his bath at night. And he never leaves the studio during the day. He just never does," said Betty. "I would think you'd know that," she added. "Or is it only Pammie you know things about?"

I was rescued from having to answer when Elsie, who had been standing there scowling, suddenly lit up with a huge grin.

"I know how to get him out of the studio."

"How?" we all asked.

"Just wait," she said. "It'll be foolproof."

"Mama's waiting for her fella. Mama's all dressed up in yella!" chanted Chester as Joanna came back to the table. Then he pointed a chubby finger at Joanna. "Hey, that's *Pammie's* dress!"

I recognized the dress as the one Mom was wearing in the *Elsie's Party* painting. Betty shot me a look.

"Is it, Connor? Do you recall it?" Betty's voice was tight. I knew she hated sensing things, yet not knowing what was going on. I'd hate it myself.

Joanna was shaking her head. "No, Chess, dear, the dress is actually mine. I just loaned it to Pamela because she didn't have anything of her own when she arrived."

"A lady of mystery," I said casually.

"Two of a kind," snapped Betty, and I knew for sure she wasn't going to let me off the hook—she was just going to wait till we were alone.

Joanna looked at me consideringly. "Betty's right. Pamela was very much of a mystery, dear, rather the way you are yourself. Appearing out of the blue to stay with us."

I looked down at my plate.

"Fitz found her out in the backyard, by the vegetable garden. Suddenly there she was, as if she'd just dropped in from the sky. She seemed to have been napping in the grass, and said she had no recollection of how she'd gotten there." Joanna pursed her lips. "Very odd."

"We think she must have been suffering from amnesia," Mrs. Cotton said. "So we let her stay with us while we made inquiries with the police. But no one had reported her missing."

"Amnesia," snorted Betty, pinching my leg hard under the table. "Must be catching."

I smacked her hand away and tried to stamp on her foot but couldn't find it.

"We were happy to have Pammie here," Joanna was saying. "We could tell she was someone of good character, even though she didn't seem to know who she was. We all liked her. But we feel bad for poor Fitzy now because he fell so madly in love. He wanted to marry her, you know."

"Poor Uncle Fitz," agreed Betty. "And now he's grumpier than ever. Always in a black mood." She tossed her brown bob. "I wish he'd find someone else to marry." Her gaze turned to rest on her mother for a moment. "Don't *you*, Mama?"

Joanna blushed. "Now, I want you children to get busy. Why not go out and have a game of ball in the yard?"

We children went out onto the porch. Elsie looked at us and puffed herself up importantly. "Ready for my plan? All right," she said. "I'll get Uncle Fitzy outside, and the rest of you rush in and find some red paint. Maybe red and a little yellow, too, so we can make our rashes look like they're oozing pus."

Betty grimaced. "You are a disgusting child, do you know that?"

"I still don't think you'll really be able to get Uncle Fitzy out of the room," said Homer. "He never comes out, not even for oozing pus."

"Ready?" Elsie grinned. "Now watch this." She took a deep breath, then ran into the house and up the stairs. We followed. In the upstairs hallway, she shoved us all into the girls' bedroom to wait, then we heard her footsteps pounding up the last flight of steps to the studio in the attic. "Uncle Fitzy! Uncle Fitzy!" we heard her cry breathlessly.

And we heard the studio door open, heard only a murmur of voices—and then there came an unearthly moan. And a shout.

"Are you sure, girl? Get out of my way!" Pounding feet coming downstairs. "Oh, my lord. Oh, yes, yes, *yes!*" Panting in the hallway as Fitzgerald Cotton stormed down the next flight as well. "My darling!" he shouted, and we heard the screen door slam.

"He's gasping like he's having a heart attack," said Chester, eyes wide.

"What in the world did she tell him?" said Betty.

"I can't imagine." Homer looked amazed.

I had a terrible suspicion I knew what Elsie had told her uncle. I peered out the window and sucked in my breath.

Homer and Chester pressed up next to me to look out, too. "He's actually outside in the garden!" said Chester. "Look at him lying there in the grass. Can you believe it?"

Then Elsie was in the doorway. *"Hurry!"* she cried. "Get upstairs and get the red and yellow paints before he comes back!"

"What did you tell him?" demanded Homer. "Why is he out there on his hands and knees?"

"Is he?" Elsie came to the window. "Oh dear. He's pounding the ground with his fists..." Her voice trailed off.

"You told him that Pamela had come back, didn't you?" I said. "You told him his muse had appeared again in the garden, just like the first time. You told him his fondest dream had come true!" I felt sort of sick.

Elsie looked abashed. "Well, yes, I did," she said. "I knew he'd run out to see her."

"But look at him!" cried Betty, her voice agonized. "I think you've practically killed him, Elsie! I think he's *crying*!"

Elsie started crying, too. "I didn't mean anything. I just wanted to get him out so we could get the red paint—"

"Look," I said, taking charge. I saw a way we might be able to put their plan *A* and my plan *B* into effect all at once—if we hurried. I didn't like to think what would happen if Fitzgerald Cotton came upstairs while we were all searching his studio. "You guys go down and see if he's okay. Elsie, you'll have to make something up...Tell him you're so sorry—you really thought you saw Pammie. It was your mama's yellow dress that fooled you... Whatever. Just hurry. And try to keep him down there, talking or something. Just go!"

They ran down the stairs. I jumped over to the girls' mirrored dressing table and searched hastily, looking into the little drawers, sifting through combs and brushes and hair ribbons until I found what I knew had to be there. Then I slid three hairpins into my hand. I ran up to the attic at top speed.

But I didn't need the hairpins—yet. The door to the studio stood open. I slipped inside and closed it behind me. I scanned the room. Little jars of paint stood on the table. I grabbed up one of red and one of yellow and stashed them in my pants pockets, then pivoted like some sort of superhero.

The room was warm and stuffy. Both the skylight and the single dormer window were open only a few inches to catch the breeze. The couch was covered in a rumpled pile of sheets and pillows. The big easel with the portrait of Mom had been moved to the corner and was once again covered by a sheet. I searched the room with my eyes. But there was no sign of the sketch, as expected. Just the big wardrobe, locked up tight. The perfect place to store sketches.

No problemo, I thought. *Bring on the locked wardrobe.*

I was like one of the coolest superheroes. Master criminals, beware! I knew there wasn't a lot of time. But if I hurried too much, I'd mess up. I wished Doug were with me. He'd appreciate the adventure. I was feeling sort of cocky—almost as if this were a game—until the breeze from the open windows lifted the sheet covering Mom's portrait on the big easel. I could see, briefly, her pink painted mouth, open in a silent scream. I fiddled with the hairpin in the lock, glancing back again at the painting.

The breeze ruffled the sheet again. Mom's mouth was stretched to the limit, straining against an unknown terror—had it been that wide a second ago?

Tears sprang to my eyes and I had to look away. Okay, so this wasn't a game.

Anyway, the first hairpin—I think it was one of those things called a bobby pin—was too thin. It had miles of room around it. It would never pick the lock. So I tried the second pin.

This one fit better. I could feel some resistance as I moved it back and forth and all around inside the lock. But there was no *click*. Nothing happened.

On to the third hairpin. I could tell this one was going to work—if only I had enough time to move it around carefully, gently, trying to sense how the lock worked....I could *feel* the sketch waiting for me inside. I thought I could feel something else waiting, too. A pulsing sort of something, waiting, wanting *out*.

A very old evil, wanting out. I lifted the hairpin out of the lock, holding my breath. I could hear my own heartbeat inside my ears.

Then I could hear something else: footsteps on the attic stairs.

This *really* wasn't a game now. I felt sick to my stomach, the big breakfast churning around like cement in a cement mixer. I wished I were just watching this on TV after all—with the remote in my hand. Time to channel surf....

But I was stuck here and now. I jumped away from the still-locked wardrobe, my heart thumping hard. I guess the good news was that Fitzgerald Cotton hadn't died of a heart attack out there in the yard when he found his muse wasn't there after all. But the bad news was—now he was just outside the door. I heard him clear his throat. I needed to hide. But where? There was no place at all. Under the couch? The gap was too narrow; only a kitten could squeeze underneath. I heard the little rasp of the door handle turning, and without thinking, I threw open the window and vaulted straight out, dropping down onto the porch roof.

I held my breath and inched my way along the roof to the side wall of the dormer. If Fitzgerald Cotton looked outside now, would he see me? I pressed myself tight against the siding.

I had to get down off the roof without anybody seeing me—and without killing myself. It was too high to jump down from the porch roof. Then I remembered there was a big tree around the back of the house. Was it close enough to the roof that I could grab a branch? I inched along, up the steep incline of the roof toward the ridge.

I could hear voices down on the porch. "Where's Connor?" That was Betty.

"He's still up there! We'd better go find him." That was Homer.

"Did he get the paints?" asked Chester.

"Oh, shut up, Chess," wailed Elsie. "This is serious! Uncle Fitzy's mad as a rattlesnake! What will happen to Connor?"

That was a very good question.

"I'll go fetch him," Homer said bravely, and I heard the screen door slam.

I could hear the scrape of the rocking chairs on the porch as the other kids waited nervously. And then I could hear Homer knocking on the studio door. "Uncle Fitz?"

I heard Fitzgerald Cotton's growl. "Can't a man get any work done around here?"

"Um, sorry, sir," mumbled Homer. "And I'm really, really sorry that Elsie thought she saw Pammie. I'm just—really, really sorry about that. But we wanted Connor—"

"You want Connor? Well, so do I! Where is that no-account stray?"

"You mean he isn't in here? We thought—"

"Haven't seen the blasted boy since the middle of the blessed night."

"Sorry, Uncle Fitz," Homer said, and from the sound of things, he hightailed it out of there. The studio door slammed. Then I heard the screen porch door slam and Homer's voice from down on the porch: "He's not up there!"

Betty sounded surprised. "Well, where is he?"

"In the bathroom?" asked Chester. "Going pee?"

"Oh no!" wailed Elsie. "Don't tell me Connor's just going to disappear the same way Pammie did!"

"*Yoo-hoo!* Connor!" Homer yelled at the top of his lungs.

I gasped and nearly slid right back down the roof.

"Connor!" They were all yelling now. "Connor, where are you? Yoo-hoo!"

"Yoo-hoo yourselves," said a different voice, and I peered over the rooftop in time to see Mr. Riley turning in at the gate. "Is someone missing?"

I thought about tossing the paint jars in my pockets down onto the grass, but there really wasn't any way the kids would be able to mix them and paint on rashes in time to convince their mother not to go out with the guy. So I just sat tight.

The kids all jumped off the porch and tried to intercept him at the gate. Betty said, "We're just looking for Connor. Our visitor. Have you seen him?"

"What are you doing here so early, anyway?" demanded Homer. "It's not lunchtime."

"I need to make several deliveries later this afternoon," Mr. Riley said. He tilted his head to look up at the trees—anything so as not to have to look at the kids, I guessed. I just hoped he wouldn't look up and see *me*. "I thought your mother and I would take our outing a bit earlier. We are going for a walk by the water and then on to an early lunch—not that it's any of your business, I might add."

"She's *our* mama, I might add," said Elsie pertly.

"Anyway," moaned Chester, "I don't think I feel so good." He clutched his stomach. "I think I have a fever. Mama! Mama!" He was off at a run, back into the house. "I'm very ill, Mama!"

Betty and Elsie went after him, and Mr. Riley followed them.

Homer stood alone, scanning the yard, no doubt trying to think where I might have gone. Then something made him look up.

"Connor!" he shouted.

I shook my head wildly and pressed my finger to my lips. Fitzgerald Cotton would be able to hear him from inside his studio. It would take only a second for him to come to the window and lean out. . . .

I fished out the two little jars of red and yellow paint and tossed them down to Homer. They landed in the bushes. He scooped them up and punched the air in victory. Then he ran into the house. I waited a minute, thinking he might have gone around the back to the tree, where they were building the fort—there was a ladder there that would come in pretty handy right about now—but he didn't come back. I figured I'd better try for the tree.

So I started edging up the roof toward the ridge. At the top of the roof was the skylight. I could see straight down into Fitzgerald Cotton's studio, and what I saw surprised me. I'd been imagining the artist furiously peering out the window—or collapsed on his couch with a heart attack—but no one was there at all. I could see the whole studio from my perch, and it was empty.

At least it was empty of the man. But the big easel had been pulled into the center of the room and the sheet was lying on the floor. One of the locked wardrobe doors now hung open, and the ancient wooden paint box was on the table directly in front of the big easel with Mom's portrait on it. He was using those special paints to paint my mom, and I could see now that her wide-stretched mouth had changed again.

Now the teeth—painted in a glistening, pearlized white—were bared. My mom had fangs!

That first slam I'd heard...that must have been the studio door. Where had old Fitzy gone? Maybe he'd gotten hungry for breakfast. Or maybe he just had to pee. I let out a high-pitched, maniacal giggle worthy of Homer. Maybe I was a little hysterical at this point.

But there I was, with the skylight open and nobody in the studio, and the ancient paint box right below me. It was a bird's-eye view. I tugged on the edge of the skylight, and it opened a little more. A kitten could squeeze through—if there had been a kitten on the roof wanting to get in. I tugged harder. The small gap widened further. Now a good-sized dog could get in. One more pull and a regular-sized boy could get in—how could I not try it?

Fitzgerald Cotton used those old paints only when painting his most important subject—my mom. If I took them, would he still paint her with regular paints? Maybe not. So it was worth a try.

I sat on the edge of the skylight and slid my legs through the opening. Then I shimmied along until my body was inside—and I dangled there, my legs waving, searching for a toehold. I guessed I could jump down and land next to the table, grab the paint box, and race out of the room before Fitzgerald Cotton finished his breakfast. Or I could climb back out the window, if necessary, and just sit there on the roof, waiting till the coast was clear. The main thing would be to have the paints in my possession.

My legs are skinny. They slipped right through—*no problemo*. But then there was a *problemo* after all. Hips, butt, torso—

Stuck!

That cement mixer was churning again, and I thought what a mess it would make on the clear glass of the skylight if I threw up all over it. Maybe Cotton would think a big bird had been passing overhead....

My heart thumped and my legs swung and I thought of Doug's dad, who did stuff like this on the tops of the highest mountains for a living. And loved it.

"Help," I whispered. Nothing happened, and no one came. But slowly, below me, the open door to the wardrobe closed. I stared down at the wardrobe and thought I could see it swelling, the doors bowing outward as if pushed by a very great presence inside. I heard a hissing sort of sound, the sound of something escaping from the wardrobe, and I held my breath because the hissing brought with it a foul smell.

Evil, I whispered.

Then both of the wardrobe doors burst open and banged closed again, hard—open, closed, open, closed!— and I could hear laughter inside my head. Although I knew it was the dumbest thing to do, I just didn't care anymore, and as the panic welled up in me I was shouting, "Help! Help! Help!" at the top of my lungs.

I heard footsteps on the stairs, but I was so totally panicked I couldn't even tell if they were coming from inside or out: porch steps or attic stairs? Then the studio door slammed open. Fitzgerald Cotton stood there, his still-wet hair standing in peaks on his head, his eyes wide with alarm. I guess it would be a freaky thing to have a voice screaming from inside the room you'd just left.... He stared up at me, and the alarm changed to amazement.

"Help?" I sort of sobbed. He just kept staring up at me. Then the amazed expression grew cunning. He was smiling—an awful smile. An evil smile. And I knew at that moment where I had seen that smile before. My blood froze.

He grabbed his sketch pad. He snatched up a stick of charcoal off the table. "Hold it right there, boy," he called. "Don't move a muscle. Okay, tip your head a little to the left—yes, just like that."

Fitzgerald Cotton was sketching me again.

∾ Chapter 13 ∾

Bloodlines

There was a huge crash—but it wasn't me falling through the skylight onto Fitzgerald Cotton and his sketch pad. No, it was—ta-dah!—*Homeboy to the rescue!* Homer slammed the studio door against the wall and stood in the doorway, hands on his hips.

"Hey, Uncle Fitzy! What about Connor?"

Uncle Fitzy just kept smiling this really awful smile. "Hay is for horses, Homer, my lad," he said slowly, rolling out the words like we had all day. "Or haven't you heard?"

Homer stepped into the room and gaped up at me. "You all right?"

I took a deep breath. "Oh, I'm hanging in there," I said. Always the funny guy, but my voice came out shaky. And my back was scraped where I'd slid through the little skylight. But the hissing was gone, the wardrobe doors were closed, and I thought the terrible sensation of evil had lessened. I could still smell the foul odor,

though, and I could feel something warm and wet trickling under my T-shirt. Blood?

Had to be. I pressed my lips together and told myself
sternly that I would *not* cry. "How's the rash?" I asked.
"Everybody feeling pretty sick down there? Any pus?"

Homer just stared up at me. "Uncle Fitzy! You have
to help Connor—he's hurt!"

"All in good time," said his uncle. "It isn't every day
a body falls from the ceiling right here in my studio, is
it? A good artist makes use of everything that comes
along." He strode over and stood under me, glaring up
through the open skylight. "Isn't that right, boy? Can
you hear me?"

Homer ran to the other side of the studio and got a
chair. He dragged the chair over while Fitzgerald Cotton
shaded the sketch with his charcoal. Homer stood upon
the chair and tugged on my feet while Fitzgerald Cotton
took his own sweet time finishing the sketch.

My shoes came off in Homer's hands. "Yow!" I yelped
through the opening. "Don't pull, Homeboy. You'll take
the rest of my skin off."

Homer let go. His uncle held the sketch pad up.
"What do you think? Is it a fair likeness? My muse has
not returned after all, and so I must take my subjects as
I find them."

I kicked my legs, hoping to make contact with his
smirking face. He caught hold of my feet and gave a
strong pull. I felt like my legs would come off. A couple
more drops of blood trickled down my back.

"Uncle Fitzy!" shouted Homer. "He's *bleeding*!"

"So he is, so he is." Fitzgerald Cotton gave me another sharp tug. "And what's a little blood between friends?" Then he stopped pulling. He stood there for a minute, considering me with that creepy smile. I felt like a beetle stuck in a spider's web. But at least a beetle would be wrapped up in soft spider gossamer. My back felt like fire.

Fitzgerald Cotton rubbed his hands over his face and scrubbed his fingers through his hair. When he looked up at me again, the awful smile was gone. It was as if there were two artists here—one with the cruel smile and actions to match, the other with a baffled expression on his face. The foul smell was gone now.

The baffled-looking Fitzgerald Cotton reached up and gripped my legs firmly. "All right now, all right, lad. Just a minute, we'll get you unstuck." He climbed on Homer's chair. "I'm going to have to push you back up, I think, rather than pull you through. Hang on."

What did he think I'd been doing all this time?

"Ready now?" he asked. "All right, then, here we go. Heave-*ho*!"

The edge of the opening scraped painfully against my back as he hoisted me up. My hands scrabbled against the shingles, trying to find something that I could use to haul myself back out onto the roof.

At last I was up. Free. I scrambled shakily onto my knees, taking in great gulps of air.

Below me I heard Fitzgerald Cotton's craggy voice: "Creep on over to the porch roof, boy. Homer's getting the ladder."

"Th—thank you," I called down to him.

"As soon as you're safely down, get yourself back up to this studio."

I swallowed hard. "Yessir." But it would be crazy to go back inside with him.

I crawled over the ridge.

"Wow!" Homer said. "You are in the biggest trouble ever!" But I saw admiration in his eyes.

I climbed down the ladder Homer held against the house. As we walked up the porch steps, I was still trying to tell myself it was stupid to go back up to the studio. Worse than stupid: dangerous. Plus, my back was killing me. I ought to be running away as fast as I could. There was no sign of Elsie or Betty or Chester, and I was glad. Then suddenly Joanna and Mr. Riley were at the front door, opening it and stepping out onto the porch.

"Oh, there you are, boys," said Joanna. She gave me a strange look, and I wondered if she'd noticed something was wrong but wasn't sure what. I guess there wasn't as much blood as I'd thought, or she'd surely see it pooling at my feet. "Betty was looking for you."

Mr. Riley focused on a spot a few feet above us. He crooked his elbow out to the side, and Joanna placed her hand on it. "Shall we go, my dear Mrs. Cotton?"

"Yes, indeed, Mr. Riley. I am looking forward to our time together."

"Uh—have fun," I called weakly.

Homer gazed after them, his shoulders drooping. "So much for plan *A*," he said dejectedly. "And Gramma says Chess has to stay in bed this afternoon with his stomachache."

"I don't think any plan *A* ever works," I said. Mine sure hadn't. And plan *B* wasn't working very well, either. It felt like hours since I'd first climbed up on the roof, but it wasn't even lunchtime. If only my mom weren't on those canvases, I'd be out of here so fast your head would spin. But she was—and so it was time for plan *C*.

Then Betty ambushed me. She materialized out of nowhere, as if she really were the ghost I thought for a moment I'd seen the night before. She grabbed my arm and hauled me into the living room. If there had been a door to slam, she'd have slammed it. But instead she just shoved me toward the couch and collapsed into the armchair across from it. Homer had followed us, and he stood there, hands on hips.

"What, Betty?" he asked. "Connor's supposed to go upstairs. He's in big trouble with Uncle Fitz."

"He's in big trouble with me," she retorted.

"Why?" Homer asked, looking from one of us to the other.

Betty heaved a huge sigh and didn't answer. I cleared my throat. "It's okay, Homer. You can go. This is between me and Betty."

"Is it?" she muttered. "I don't think so. I think your lies ought to be of interest to the whole family."

"'Lies'?" repeated Homer. His eyes narrowed. "We don't like liars around here."

"Oh, shut up, Homeboy," I snapped, and I was suddenly so furious with everybody I just felt like screaming.

I couldn't fight this war on all fronts. I was here to save Mom, and that's what I had to concentrate on. I was going to get kicked out of the house, anyway, now, after the morning's fiasco on the roof...and I still didn't have that sketch, and I still hadn't stolen that old paint box, and worst of all there was something unspeakable up in that studio, inside the wardrobe. Mom was endangered by it, and so was I, and so, probably, were all the Cottons. So why *not* just tell Betty and Homer the truth— not just to get them off my back, but to enlist their help?

"All right already," I said resolutely. "I *have* been lying to you. But only because the truth is so weird I can hardly believe it myself."

"Try us," said Betty calmly. She got up out of the chair and came over to sit next to me on the couch. "Tell us, Connor," she urged in her most sensible voice. "I know you have secrets. I don't believe you're an orphan who has been wandering the streets! You're too *clean,* for one thing. And your clothes are...strange. Your shoes. Well, you just don't fit in, somehow. I want you to tell us everything."

I looked straight at Betty. I could see the green flecks in her eyes. "I'll tell you a story."

"Is it *Star Wars*?" asked Homer.

"No," I said. "But it's also about good fighting evil." And then I took a deep breath. "First of all, your *Pammie* is my *mother*. I know, I know," I said quickly, as Homer's mouth opened to interrupt me. "I know she was your uncle's muse and everything, but before that—

before she ever even *heard* of you—she was my mom. And she still is." I was trying to feel my way into the story. How much to tell and how much to leave out? "Her name is Pamela Rigoletti." I saw Betty's mouth drop open, but I hurried on. "She's a lawyer. My dad's into computers—well, never mind; I know you don't know what those are. It doesn't matter. Anyway, his name is Grant Chase. I know, different names—but that's how married people sometimes do it in my, uh, *area*. And Pamela and Grant, they have two kids—me and my sister, Crystal. Crystal is your age, Betty."

Homer crossed his arms and rolled his eyes. Betty cleared her throat. "Rigoletti? Pammie told us she couldn't remember her last name."

"Maybe she couldn't." I drew in a big breath. That had been the easy part. Now for the really impossible stuff.

"We live here in Shady Grove, but not in 1926."

"Not—" Betty broke in. Then she shook her head.

"I know it sounds impossible," I hurriedly continued. "But we're, like, about eighty years in the future. Don't ask me how these two times exist at the same time! All I know is, they do—and your house stands where our house will be built one day. And one day my mom will open an old art book and find a sketch inside, a sketch by the famous artist Fitzgerald Cotton."

"Famous!" said Homer. "You liar."

"It's the truth, and it already happened," I said stiffly. "My mom somehow found a sketch that your uncle had drawn long ago, though she didn't know that then—and she must have been freaked out, because the sketch was of *her*. I sure was freaked out, anyway, when I saw it. And when I touched it, a cold wind started blowing..."

I told the whole story, not even caring—right then—whether they believed me. It was just such a relief to tell them who I really was and how I'd come to be there. I told as much of the story as I'd figured out. That somehow Mom had come here and stayed a year and been Fitzgerald Cotton's muse, and then somehow she'd come home again, right to the time she'd left. I knew that had to be true, because otherwise we would have missed her. I hoped if I ever got home that I, too, would return to the minute I left. It would be terrible if all the time I was here, Mom and Dad were worrying about me and calling the police to file a missing person report and everything.

"So that's what I was doing up in your uncle's studio," I concluded. "Looking for the sketch so I can go home again. You guys want to help me find it?"

Homer just stood there, shaking his head. He looked sad, or sort of betrayed. "I thought you were my friend, Connor," he said. "But time travel? That's as made up as space travel. You're telling us to believe in fairy tales. Or saying that...Luke Skywalker...is real!"

"I'm not saying Luke Skywalker is real," I said. "I'm saying *magic* is real." So was space travel, actually, but I wasn't about to try telling them that.

Homer snorted. "Prove it!"

Betty looked at me intently. "*Can* you prove it? Prove you're from the future, I mean?"

I shrugged. It wasn't like I had an ID card or anything showing my birth date, and I didn't even have any money on me—except, of course, for the quarter Fitzgerald Cotton had given me. If only I had a coin from my own time, so I could show the year engraved on it.... I fished in my pockets and came up with Doug's key chain. I tightened my fingers around the metal Death Star and drew it out to show them. The red light flashed in my hand. It didn't really prove anything, but they both stared down at it openmouthed.

"Look," Betty finally said. "Even if the magic is real, Uncle Fitz isn't a magician. He's just a painter. So how does he have the power to pull your mom to our time?"

"I don't know," I said slowly. "That's what I've been trying to find out."

Then Betty went up to her bedroom and came back down with the big book she'd borrowed from her uncle. She sat down and paged through till she came to the portrait of Francesca Rigoletti.

"The last name," she said slowly, running her finger over the text. "It must mean *something*."

"And the lady looks like Pammie, too," added Homer, coming over to look at the book.

I moved closer to Betty on the couch so I could check out the picture again. It was eerie seeing the resemblance to Mom in the old portrait, and strange to see the name Rigoletti on the page. "My mom hasn't ever been to

Italy, I'm pretty sure," I said. "But I know her ancestors came from there. My ancestors, I guess. Generations ago. What if—what if we're related to *this* Rigoletti in the picture? That would be a connection, wouldn't it?"

"A connection to this portrait, but not to Uncle Fitz," Betty pointed out. "If the magic was about an old connection to Italy, why wouldn't she be pulled back in time to when this portrait was painted or something?"

I didn't know, but I felt absolutely sure the connection between Mom and Francesca Rigoletti mattered.

I turned the page and stared down at the group of portraits the Magi Painters had painted of one another. As before, the portrait of Lorenzo da Padova stood out. The leering face was so unpleasant—and yet the text reported that he had been the most gifted of the group of artists. I studied his face a moment longer, then turned back to the page with Francesca Rigoletti's portrait and my heart started thumping harder. I read the text next to her portrait: *Francesca Rigoletti, 1479. Painted by Lorenzo da Padova, of the Magi School.* And, sure enough, down in the corner of the portrait, there was a tiny sketch of a smiling face.

I grew cold, as if the spring day had turned to winter. My lips felt stiff as I opened my mouth to speak. "What if it's him?" I said, and my voice came out sounding as hoarse as it had the day I'd arrived from my own time. "What if the paints in the paint box upstairs belonged to Lorenzo da Padova for sure, not just to any one of the Magi Painters?"

"And da Padova had used the same ones to paint Francesca Rigoletti," breathed Betty.

"And your uncle is related to Lorenzo da Padova. And my mother is somehow related to Francesca Rigoletti..."

My voice trailed off and I turned the page back to the portraits of the Magi School. Lorenzo da Padova sneered at me off the page. I felt shaken. The magic was older than I'd supposed, the evil deeper. The book said that Lorenzo da Padova had died in 1479—the same year he had painted Francesca Rigoletti—but I had a terrible feeling he was still, in some way, very much alive even now.

Betty leaned over the book and read aloud. "Listen to this! 'Da Padova's work was so impressive that he was sought after by princes. Yet there were rumors about him that never died away: that he had poisoned his family, that he had swindled his neighbors out of their fortunes, that he treated his models harshly, that he dabbled in black magic. Nothing was ever proven. Da Padova died at age twenty-nine, stabbed through the heart by an unknown assailant—possibly someone who wanted revenge. After the artist's death, his fellow Magi Painters kept his belongings because no family member came forth to claim them. His paintings were later sold to museums throughout Italy and the rest of the world.'"

"They kept his belongings!" I said, and it was as if a bell went off in my head, and I was remembering what Fitzgerald Cotton had said the day before, up in his studio, about paints getting old, growing sour. I'd felt then I was on the edge of understanding something important, but that something had eluded me. Now it was slowly coming clear.

"They sold Lorenzo da Padova's paintings to museums," I said softly, "but what did they do with his *stuff*? His painting stuff?"

The paints he used had some magical properties, I felt sure of it, as sure as I was of anything. I didn't know *how*, but somehow those paints were holding my mom captive. Whether Fitzgerald Cotton was an evil magician or just a painter who didn't know his own power, he was using paints that were capturing her soul. Mom's very life was at stake every time Fitzgerald Cotton lifted his brush to canvas. It wouldn't be enough just to steal the paint box, as I had thought.

"Those paints have to be gotten rid of for good," I said. "They have to be destroyed."

I heard a hissing sound from the corner of the room and craned my neck to see what was there.

Nothing.

Betty was nodding. "I think you're right." She bent over the book again. "And it says here that Francesca Rigoletti was Lorenzo da Padova's muse." She looked up, frowning.

"But that doesn't prove anything," Homer objected. "Our last name isn't da Padova!" He crossed his arms. "I don't want to be related to a creepy fellow like that."

"I'm not saying we're directly related—but it makes sense," Betty said quietly. "The name wouldn't be the same as ours because we have the name Cotton, after Grandpa. The Italian connection would be through Gramma. What matters is that there's a real connection—and somehow they're playing out the same story over again. Da Padova and his muse."

We all stared at one another. I felt a prickle on the back of my neck as though the unseen presence from the wardrobe had entered the room. The silence stretched across time.

Homer wrinkled his nose. "What's that awful smell?"

PART THREE

Revenge

And when many weeks had passed...the
painter stood entranced before the work...
and crying with a loud voice, "This is indeed
Life itself!" turned suddenly to regard his
beloved: —She was dead!

— EDGAR ALLAN POE,
"The Oval Portrait"

Padua, Italy. August 1479

The Smiler's thin lips twisted with pleasure. But when he peered around the canvas on his easel for another look at his model, his smile turned into a fierce frown. His muse had drooped on her brocade bench in the heat. He looked at her with distaste.

On the canvas she appeared bright and fresh, dewy in her eternal beauty and loveliness. In person, however, she looked anything but bright or fresh these days. She had grown irritatingly sallow and wan, also much thinner than when they'd begun. Her wracking cough had been a constant source of annoyance for weeks now, because it caused her to shudder, thus disturbing the pose. But a measured dose from the dagger's secret compartment—mixed into her wine to conceal the bitter taste— had brought blessed silence. Sometimes she drooped so alarmingly these days that even his sharp words or hard slap would not revive the pose, and he needed to take firmer measures, even going so far one day as to secure her into position with lengths of fabric, hoisting her into place. Sometimes she would not hold the rose properly— but he had finished that portion of the painting some weeks ago. Now he didn't need to use a flower anymore at all, but still he liked having her hold it. *Making* her hold it.

Bending her to his will.

Today her cousin was coming to convey her back to their home near Venice. Today he would have to pay her for her services—he hated to part with any of his gold, but models were not easy to come by anymore. And of course he did not want just any model. He wanted—no, *needed*—this particular beauty.

She should have been his from the start, of course.

He left his stool and pulled his money box from the shelf behind him. He counted out the gold ducats and laid them on the table. "You see them?" he asked the girl. "They are yours, as soon as we are done."

She did not answer him, but he had become used to that.

"As soon as we are done," he repeated. "Then you shall return to Venice with your good cousin. You will

see your baby again. You will see your friends again."
He often spoke this way to keep her spirits high and to
make her eyes sparkle. But they had not held a sparkle in
many days now. It was most disagreeable.

Oh! The light was changing as the afternoon wore
on, and he must keep working if he were to finish the last
strokes before the cousin arrived. He did not care to be
hurried! How dare any man try to hurry Lorenzo da
Padova?

He listened for hoofbeats as he mixed a new batch of
tempera. The paint must be perfectly smooth, the color
deep and even. He unscrewed the cap of his dagger and
sprinkled the poison liberally into the mixture, stirring it
well. This extra ingredient was essential. He sifted goodly
amounts of it into each bag of powdered pigment, but always liked to add just a touch more to the fresh paint.
And now...*Perfetto!*

He heard shuffles outside the open windows as the
servants went about their work. One of the servants broke
into a snatch of song—but it was quickly stifled. All the
servants should know quite well by now that he required
silence—and solitude—for his work.

Meals were left punctually outside his studio door,
covered by white linen to keep away the bugs and rats.
Often he forgot to eat and was reminded only when his
muse begged for sustenance. Eventually she had grown
so quiet, days might pass when she did not speak at all.

These past few days, she'd eaten nothing. He frowned
at her again over the top of the canvas. Yes, she'd become

a wreck of a woman—a mere shadow of the Francesca Rigoletti who had first stepped through the studio door. It was most vexing.

But, no matter. The painting was the thing. The painting was what mattered! He gazed upon his work with the utmost satisfaction and pride.

Layer upon layer, colors mixed to perfection, their hues luminous on the canvas, their depth amazing even to him who mixed and applied them. A special magic came over him as he worked. This was his finest painting ever.

Hark! The sounds of hoofbeats and voices. A rider had entered the courtyard and was greeted by the servants. There came a knocking on the door. But he could not answer just yet—there was work still to be finished. The painting was not done! *Go away!* he thought but did not call out aloud. *Let me finish! You must not hurry the Master!*

The knocking changed to pounding, and then the door to the chamber burst open. His manservant tried to close it again, speaking rapidly to the intruder that the artist must not be interrupted. But the man shoved him aside and strode into the room.

"Lorenzo da Padova?" cried the man who entered. "I am Giovanni Compianno, come for my cousin, the lady Francesca!"

Lorenzo could not answer, he was working so intently. Just this last little bit...just this last little bit...

"Great God, man! What is this?" cried Giovanni Compianno, running across the studio to where his cousin sat lashed into position with a long, white scarf knotted tightly across her torso. "What madness is this?" He pulled out his knife and began sawing at the restraint.

Just this last little shadow on her delicate face, and— *Perfètto!* The painting needed only the signature. The signature of Il Sorridente.

The model fell into her cousin's arms. "Is she dead, man? Have you killed her? By God, if she is—"

In the lower right-hand corner of the large canvas the little face of a smiling man took shape under Lorenzo da Padova's brush. The face was nearly hidden by the folds of Francesca's skirts in the painted shadows—but it was there.

Too late, Lorenzo looked up just as the raging man descended upon him, knife thrusting in vengeful fury. Too late to grab his own dagger, so sharp and ready, but tucked out of sight. Too late—

The Smiler fell to the stone floor. His blood spilled out into the shaft of late-afternoon sunlight. He struggled to speak. He cried out, "Death cannot hold me! I shall live on in my paint!" Then he fixed his eye on the canvas he knew in his heart was his very finest work—his masterpiece. And he whispered, "My muse...my muse...I shall paint you till the end of time!" even as he drew his last earthly breath.

∽ *Chapter 14* ∽

Shapes and Shadows

*F*itzgerald Cotton's booming voice calling from the studio came as a huge relief: "Where are you, you young hooligan? Connor? Get up here!"

I went up the stairs to the attic. Every step sent a stab of pain across my scraped back. Betty carried the book as she and Homer climbed behind me.

I told myself the important thing—the *only* thing— was to get my hands on that ancient paint box. Fitzgerald Cotton—or Lorenzo da Padova—had to be stopped from controlling my mom. So my scraped back stung—so what? The pain only made me braver.

Showdown time.

But back inside the studio again, I saw something that sent a jolt right up my spine and erased every bit of braveness: The big easel with the painting of Mom was right in front of me. And there was Fitzgerald Cotton, holding the ancient paint box, shaking powdered pigment from a pouch into his mixing bowl. The painting showed Mom's anguished face, her frozen eyes—same as before. But her mouth, open in a scream, seemed wider than it had been when I last looked at it. The white teeth glistened. I could almost feel Mom trembling with trying to move out of her frozen pose—and suddenly I could hear her thoughts, really *hear* them in my head: *Connor, quickly—he's killing me!*

"Stop!" I shouted. And Fitzgerald Cotton spun around.

"You owe me thanks for the rescue, an apology for the intrusion, and an explanation of your abominable behavior, boy," he said, his eyes narrowing. "Not more histrionics."

I didn't know what histrionics were, and I didn't care. "Just stop painting my mother!" I ordered in a voice that came out rough and hard. "Stop it right now."

"Your mother?" demanded Fitzgerald Cotton. His face turned red. But he did set the paint box down on the table. "Did I hear you say your *mother*?"

"He means Pammie," said Homer.

"Connor's told us everything," Betty said to her uncle. "I *knew* that he knew Pammie."

I felt relieved to have Betty and Homer with me, facing down Fitzgerald Cotton in his studio—the beast in his lair—as if their presence would ward off whatever evil lurked here.

"My beautiful muse?" whispered Fitzgerald Cotton.

"Yes, your *muse*." I was keeping my eye on the paint box while I talked, edging closer and closer to the table.

Little baby steps, like maybe if I was real slow and stealthy, Fitzy wouldn't notice.

Fitzgerald Cotton's heavy hand descended on my shoulder. "Sit down. Tell me everything. Everything, boy! How can my beloved muse be your mother when you're an orphan? Or—do you mean to say that Pamela is *dead*?" His red cheeks paled. His eyes were wild but not in a crazy way—just scared. Scared for my mom. And suddenly I realized that deep inside he didn't mean to hurt her. Maybe he didn't even know he *was* hurting her!

"She's not dead," I told him. "But she will be soon if you don't stop painting her."

"If I don't stop painting—" He shook his shaggy head.

"If you really don't know what I'm talking about," I began, "then you probably don't know how much you're hurting her, and you're not as horrible as I've been thinking you are. As horrible as *she* thinks you are."

A spasm of pain crossed his face. "She doesn't think I'm horrible! She loves me—"

"Look at that portrait and say she looks like someone in love!" I shouted, pointing to the easel. "She's terrified of you because you keep painting her—with these." I reached over and snatched up the old wooden box of paints. The box was surprisingly heavy. It was as if the paint pouches inside were weighted with all their years. Or with their magic.

"Don't touch those, boy!" Fitzgerald Cotton barked at me. "I told you they're precious!"

I hung on tightly and turned away from him. "Yes, you did. You told me yourself the legend of how powerful these paints are, how they belonged to the old masters and are supposed to have special—maybe magical—properties. Well, it's true! They do! They really do! In fact, they're Lorenzo da Padova's own paints, and their magic is so powerful, it is reaching right through time."

"I confess to being completely baffled." Fitzgerald rubbed his hands over his face and looked beseechingly at his nephew and niece. "Homer? Betty? Do you two know what all this madness is about?" He was either the best actor ever, or else he really was innocent. I just couldn't tell which it was.

"Sort of." Homer's eyes were shining with excitement.

"We have a theory," Betty admitted. "But you're not going to like it, Uncle Fitz."

"Our theory is that there's something wrong with your old paints," Homer burst out.

"They have to be destroyed," I said, hanging on to the paint box.

"'Destroyed,' you say?" repeated Fitzgerald Cotton in a casual voice. Then he suddenly grabbed for the box, spinning me around so that I collapsed onto the couch in a slump. So he wasn't innocent! I clutched the paint box, holding on for dear life.

The portrait of Mom stared down at me. I turned my face away. "They're evil!" I shouted up at Fitzgerald Cotton. I heard tears behind my voice and I hated that—but I couldn't help it. "Either they are . . . or *you* are."

That stopped him. "Evil?" he hissed. Homer and

Betty were standing behind their uncle—Homer's eyes wide and scared, Betty's narrowed.

"*Evil,*" I confirmed. "Because whenever you paint my mom with these paints, you have power over her. The paints let you reach through time and capture her. She's like a zombie—frozen. Scared out of her mind, and she can't move. She gets like a statue. She goes into a trance."

"Did you say 'through time'?" Fitzgerald Cotton looked stunned for a moment. Then his expression changed, as if someone had drawn a brush over it and painted in something new. He looked crafty; he looked cunning. He reached again for the box.

I wrapped my arms around it. *Oh no, you don't.*

"You're killing her," I whispered. Tears pricked my eyelids, but no way was I going to let him see me cry.

Fitzgerald Cotton lunged again for the paint box, but Betty grabbed him from behind. "No," she said. "Wait." Then she pulled him down to sit next to me on the couch. "Maybe we should tell him the story. The facts of the matter."

"Oh yes, indeed," he said. "I love a good tale." He glanced over at me and his smile was cold—and dreadfully familiar.

I shivered. "I don't think I need to tell him anything," I said to Betty. "I think he knows. In fact, maybe…"

"Maybe what, lad?" pressed Fitzgerald Cotton, and it seemed to me even the air in the room was changing. Something had *shifted*. There was a little hissing sound in the air, and I felt the same presence I'd sensed downstairs in the living room. The same presence from the wardrobe. The cold little smile I hated was playing about Fitzgerald Cotton's lips.

I took a deep breath. "Maybe you *knew*," I said. "I think you've known all along that the old paints have a special magic. And you know they're holding my mom hostage. But maybe you even knew back when you first bought these old paints that they belonged to Lorenzo da Padova! Maybe bad things happened to people who used da Padova's paints, and other artists knew the paints were dangerous, or sour, or bad, and so that's why they were never used up in all those years. The paints survived so many centuries because no one *dared* to use them!"

"Until me," said Fitzgerald Cotton softly, and the smile grew wider.

"Until you." I took a deep breath because I had to say it: "He's got you in his power."

"Nonsense." The smile disappeared. "Look here, boy. I admit I did learn that the paints belonged to da Padova before I bought them—but so what? Why shouldn't I purchase old paints if I want them? They're the paints of a master painter, my own ancestor. I am honored to own them, and I only wish I could paint as brilliantly as da Padova did!" Fitzgerald Cotton bowed his head like he was praying or something.

"The man was evil," I snapped.

"Or totally mad," Betty added, pointing to a page in the art book. "At least, people thought he was."

Fitzgerald lifted his head. "The man has been dead for centuries. You're delusional, you kids. As mad as da Padova was said to be. And so what if the man was crazy? He was an artist! He was a marvel! People feared and revered him—they recognized his genius. He was known by his code name in the Magi School, Il Sorridente. The Smiler." Fitzgerald Cotton's voice became distant, dreamy. "His smile was something awful to see, I've read—frightening. Vengeful. He liked to sign his paintings with that smile. You'd have to search carefully through a crowd scene or a host of angels or whatever it was that he'd painted, and you'd find a face with da Padova's own vicious smile."

"Like this," murmured Betty, her finger tapping the picture of Francesca Rigoletti's portrait in the art book.

It was the artist's little joke, I thought. Sort of like how Alfred Hitchcock found it fun to appear in his own movies. But Hitchcock only made scary movies; he himself wasn't scary in real life. Lorenzo da Padova *was* scary in real life. And I had the feeling he was still alive—somehow—and right here with us in the room.

"I don't want to be related to him, Uncle Fitz," Homer piped up.

"It doesn't matter," I said quickly to Homer. "You've got the genes of loads of other ancestors in you that cancel him out."

"'Genes'?" asked Homer, perplexed.

"Never mind," I said hurriedly. "What really matters is the paints. Your uncle's got da Padova's paints—and that's why da Padova's got your uncle." I slapped my open palms down hard on the wooden paint box and turned to look Fitzgerald Cotton full in the face. "And that's why *you've* got my mom!"

"What Connor's saying," breathed Betty at my side, "is that you're *possessed*, Uncle Fitz." I felt her arm tremble against mine.

"Nonsense!" barked Fitzgerald Cotton, his eyes glittering.

I pointed a shaking finger at the shocking portrait of Mom. "What's that, then? Whose signature is *that*?"

It was hard to see, at first, but it was there—hidden down in the shadows of the right-hand corner of Fitzgerald Cotton's largest canvas, painted with Fitzgerald Cotton's own hand: the sly, smiling face of a little man.

PART FOUR

Life after Death

*For those whom thou think'st thou dost
   overthrow,
Die not, poor Death, nor yet canst thou
   kill me.*

—JOHN DONNE,
Holy Sonnets

Padua, Italy. September 1479

The funeral was over, and three painters of the Magi School gathered back at Lorenzo da Padova's studio. They were the ones who lived in closest proximity to his villa, so they were the ones who had to come empty the artist's chamber of all the man's possessions.

The sumptuous villa in Padua now belonged to the young wife, whom da Padova had abandoned many years earlier. She and her fatherless children would soon move in. But the widow wanted nothing to do with the art studio.

In fact, the young widow had sent word via messenger that the artwork could be burned for all she cared. God forbid she would ever hang any of da Padova's paintings in her home! *Dio mio!*

Burn the paintings? The Magi Painters were aghast. Never! They had not liked the painter—indeed, many in their group had feared him—but no one could discount his genius. The Magi Painters knew the paintings would fetch the widow a fine price. High-placed ministers of government were interested in the collection of landscapes, and the prince who had already commissioned several portraits would most happily purchase any others for his private gallery. The Magi Painters arranged for the sales. Now these three surveyed the nearly empty studio.

There were the props da Padova had used to set the stage for his paintings: the lengths of velvet, the bowls for fruit, the etched wine goblets. "I will take all these," said Guiseppe Sebastiani. "Il Sorridente would want me to have them, I feel sure."

"Well, I can use his blank canvases," Marcello d'Augustino piped up. "And these carved wooden easels to put them on. I know he would be most pleased for me to have them."

"Then I shall take the model's chair," pronounced Julio Luciano, indicating the brocade bench where Lorenzo da Padova had posed his subjects. "And this little table. His soul will rest easier, knowing I am putting them to daily use."

The men carried their new possessions to the door,

then turned back to regard the room uneasily. Something did not feel quite right.

Nothing was left now but da Padova's jars of supple brushes, his palette, and a carved wooden box full of pigments. Yet no one had rushed to claim these things. No one seemed to want to touch them at all.

The artists coughed nervously. Julio Luciano reached for the door handle, but the door would not open. The men had left it unlocked when they entered, all three were quite certain of this. But now it was stuck firmly, as if bolted from the outside.

The three men pulled hard on the handle, twisting it to the right and to the left. A faint, foul-smelling breeze wafted through the room, though the window was tightly closed. The men banged the door with their fists to alert the servants. But still no one came, and the men felt their growing unease turn to dread. Then—

"Hark!" gasped Marcello d'Augustino, holding up one finger so the others would stop banging and listen.

"What is it that I hear?" stammered Julio Luciano. The three men held their breath, waiting, listening. From the far side of the room there came a faint hissing noise. And then the scraping sound of something sliding...

The wooden paint box on the table was sliding slowly toward the edge, pushed by some unseen force. The three men drew back in terror when the box reached the table's edge yet did not fall. They backed against the door as the paint box floated toward them, drifting like a feather in the air. Marcello d'Augustino bravely reached out his two hands and took hold of the box as it neared him.

"I think," he said weakly, "I shall take this paint box. Il Sorridente would want me to."

The three men stared at one another, breathing heavily.

"Yes, indeed," whispered Julio Luciano.

"His memory will never die," Guiseppe Sebastiani spoke up brightly, his voice loud in the small room.

"Indeed not," agreed Marcello d'Augustino quickly. "And these paints will always enjoy a place of honor on my shelf. Even when I am dead and buried, these paints will remain! I have heard tell that the pigments of famous artists fetch very high prices at auction. I have no doubt the paints in this box will someday be bought by someone who will appreciate their history and the brilliance of their original owner."

The artists glanced at one another. They stood still, waiting. Then they pulled the handle on the door to the studio—and it opened quite easily now. In their panic they left behind everything in the studio they had planned to take. Everything—except the carved, wooden paint box.

Unpleasant laughter, borne on a foul-smelling breeze, followed them as they escaped into the sunlit courtyard.

∽ Chapter 15 ∽

Showdown

Fitzgerald Cotton reeled in shock when he saw the little face painted down in the corner of the portrait of Mom. *He really didn't know! I* thought, but ignorance was no excuse.

Fitzgerald Cotton rubbed his eyes. He took a deep breath, glanced at the signature face on the ugly portrait, then away, then back again as if he really couldn't believe it was there. As if he hadn't been the one to paint it there himself.

"This rather changes things," he murmured. "Indeed, I think it does. I thought you were out of your mind, lad," he said, looking over at me now with something like wonder in his usually fierce eyes. "But..."

"But you didn't know you'd painted the face?" asked Betty in a hopeful voice.

"I didn't know," he said. "It puts a rather different...ah, *face*...on things. If you'll pardon the pun. It's very strange indeed. I have felt odd ever since I began using the ancient paints. They exert a—a *spell*, you might call it. I paint better than ever when I'm using them. I feel a very compelling...ah, *power*."

He collapsed onto the couch and put his face in his hands. "When I returned from Italy some time back, I'd carefully stored away the special paints I'd purchased at such great expense. But then one day I ran out of inspiration. I lacked the drive to paint—felt all my subjects had been exhausted. It's a terrible feeling for an artist, I tell you, to feel so *blocked*. So empty of passion and drive. For months I did not paint! Then one day I decided that maybe using the special paints would give me some new ideas...and so I opened the box and started to mix the dry pigments the way the old masters had—using a fresh egg yolk...That's the first time I felt it. The power."

He stopped talking into his hands and raised his head to look at Homer and Betty and me. "When I finished mixing the paints, all was ready. I was motivated, excited again—except I still had no fitting subject. It seemed to me that paints like these needed a very special person posing for a portrait. I walked to the window and stared down—amazingly a vision came to me, a vision of my next subject. Quickly I snatched up my sketch pad and a stick of charcoal, and I started trying to sketch what my mind was imagining—the loveliest woman in the world down there in the garden. I imagined her sitting on lush grass, a smile lighting her eyes, her hand lifted toward me as if in welcome or desire...and that's the way I drew her."

That was *the* sketch! The one I'd been searching for. But where was it now?

"*Ahhhh.*" He shook his head dreamily. "When I had completed the sketch, I stared at it a long time. Then something made me look out the window again—and that's when I saw her."

"Saw who?" I asked, but somehow I knew what was coming.

"I looked down, and I could see into the garden," Fitzgerald Cotton repeated in a dazed voice. "And there— what do you suppose?—I saw the figure of a woman lying on the grass by the vegetable garden." He took a deep breath. "And not just any woman! The most ethereal, most exquisite, most *paintable* woman in the whole world. The very woman I had just sketched!"

Betty glanced out the window. "I don't think you could really see much of a person from way up here, Uncle Fitzy. Not really."

"I could see every hair on her head," he insisted. "It was the same woman I had invented with my sketch, and I knew I must paint her. Clearly this was my muse. I had conjured her up, and she was meant to be mine."

"It was Pammie," said Homer. "Let's see the sketch you did of her, Uncle Fitzy."

"Yes—please?" added Betty.

Fitzgerald Cotton's eyes fastened on mine. When he spoke, his voice shook. "I ran downstairs and out into the garden. There she was, lying on the grass. My fingers actually itched, I tell you. Itched to hold a brush and start painting again. It was a wonderful feeling—heaven-sent."

I could picture it perfectly, like it was happening on video. Like I'd been here that day.

"She sat up and looked so confused—reaching out her hand to me, asking where she was. She smiled at me then, and looked exactly like the sketch. But when I asked her how she'd come to be here in our garden, she seemed not to know. I told her she must be my muse, sent from heaven to inspire me! She came inside and had dinner with us. She knew her name was Pamela—but she still couldn't remember anything else about who she was or how she'd come to be in our garden. My parents pressed her for details, but I knew it didn't matter. A magical creature such as she could not have come from the ordinary world."

Mom, I was thinking. *My ordinary, precious mom.*

"I painted her every morning, using the old paints. I was painting better than ever before. Soon it felt like she'd always been with us. She made herself right at home with my parents and Joanna. You kids adored her—right, Homer, my lad? Betty?"

"She was the bee's knees," Homer agreed readily.

"She was very nice," said Betty. "But I could tell she was sad inside."

"She was happy with us," the artist went on, ignoring Betty. "I was pleased she had amnesia. Sometimes she started saying it was time for her to go home—but I'd get a terrible panicky feeling, and I'd say, *'Just one more painting, my love, just one more!'* And she'd agree, and then she'd be happy here again and wouldn't be talking of leaving us. As long as I painted her, she stayed. And everything I painted of her was a success. I started entering my work in shows. I was asked to exhibit in galleries all over the state. Collectors came from all around the country last fall—some even from Europe! It was amazing, and I owed my success, my moments of glory, to my lovely muse. But then, one day—"

He fell silent, staring at the awful painting on the big easel. I sat quietly, my arms wrapped around the paint box, hardly daring to breathe.

"One day I fell ill," he said simply. "I was sick for weeks, and I could not paint her. Couldn't lift a brush. At first she brought my food on a tray, tried to help nurse me . . . But then she stopped coming. Joanna or my mother came instead. I asked for my muse. I cried out for her! They told me . . . told me she had left." Fitzgerald Cotton snapped his fingers. "Gone. Just like that. My life was over." He buried his face in his hands again.

"She came home to us," I murmured, my eyes on him.

"I searched everywhere," Fitzgerald Cotton confided, lifting his head. "Until finally even I had to admit she was really gone. So I tried to paint her anyway, tried to pick up where I'd left off before my illness—I figured I could just envision her, paint from memory . . . And of course I would use my best paints, the way I always had. To honor her."

We sat staring at the grotesque painting. No honor there. None at all.

"Now look at her," groaned Fitzgerald Cotton.

"Sweet Pamela, what have I done to you?" He clutched his head as if it ached. "It was never my intention to hurt you, my love. You must believe me. I can't bear to be the cause of your unhappiness."

I couldn't decide who this man next to me really was—an evil madman or a humbled, grieving artist. From one minute to the next I could believe he was either or neither—or both.

Fitzgerald Cotton tore his anguished eyes from the awful portrait and jumped up off the couch again. "Every time I try to paint her, it comes out looking monstrous," he cried. "I've been trying and trying and making myself crazy trying to get it right—it was so easy before!—but in every single painting now, she looks just terrible." He picked up a brush and jabbed at the canvas. "And yet, I *must* paint her!"

He looked like he might cry, for a second or two.... But then suddenly he was looking really different again, as if that invisible brush had swept across his face and replaced sadness with slyness. The eyes narrowed, the eyebrows quirked up. The mouth twisted into a crafty sneer—the smile of a different man entirely.

"You must *not* paint her," Betty said quietly. "For your own sanity, Uncle Fitzy."

"And for hers," I added. "Never again." My own words sent a shiver down my back, because I knew now what I was going to have to do to make things right.

Betty stood up, still holding the art book. "Francesca Rigoletti is somehow connected to Pammie. They even have the same last name! We think she must be a direct ancestor, linked through their bloodline all through the centuries, linking Connor, too. We think that since Lorenzo da Padova can't have his original muse, he'll take one who looks like Francesca Rigoletti! Someone who is related to her. And you're related to *him,* Uncle Fitz."

"Not just related to him," I corrected. "You're *becoming* him."

Fitzgerald Cotton snorted, a most unpleasant sound. "Utter nonsense. Pure rot."

"We think you're possessed by Lorenzo da Padova against your will!" cried Homer.

"Either that, Uncle Fitz, or you're *letting* it happen. We think you're very wrong to let him use you this way." Betty crossed her arms and stared at her uncle angrily. "And we won't let you do it anymore."

Before Fitzgerald Cotton could answer, Betty turned to me with a look of such intensity that I was sure she wanted to say something more. Taking her look as my signal, I flew into action.

I darted off the couch, the paint box tight in my grasp.

Fitzgerald Cotton lunged after me. I knocked over mason jars of brushes, and tipped a tin can onto the floor in my haste to get away. The stink of turpentine made my eyes water as I ducked away from him. "Betty!" I yelled. "Hey, Betty!"

I tossed her the paint box, right over Homer's head, and she caught it neatly. She should be on a football team, that girl, except that in 1926 girls didn't play football.

Fitzgerald Cotton was wheezing as he turned and leaped at his niece. Betty flung the paint box back to me just as he reached her, and he toppled forward onto the couch. I ran over to the small porcelain sink in the corner of the room.

I turned on one tap; I opened the box. And then Fitzgerald Cotton was up again, and he was on me. I tried to kick him away, but he grabbed my arms. Then Betty was there, too, pulling him off me.

"Not down the drain!" he howled as I opened the wooden box. "I need them! Even after everything, I *need* them!" But I dumped the little bags out into the sink.

Homer and Betty stood clutching his arms, holding him back as I fumbled to loosen the ties and let the colored powders run away under the pounding water. Cobalt blue. Deepest crimson. Sea green. Two different yellows, purple, brown, gray—and darkest black.

Some of the black paint splashed up out of the sink—onto the back of my hand—burning like a brand.

"Down the drain!" wailed Fitzgerald Cotton. "No—not down the drain!"

"Hey! Oh, hey, looky here!" screeched Homer, with such a note of panic that even his uncle was silenced, and we all immediately wheeled to look where he was pointing. The large portrait of Mom on the easel was shuddering ever so slightly, as if a mild earthquake were rumbling miles beneath the house. The deep thick paint was fading.

And then all of a sudden there was another face there, another face under the paint. It was the face I'd glimpsed in Fitzgerald Cotton's own, but vivid now, nothing shadowy about it. And I realized that Fitzgerald Cotton had been held prisoner just as surely as my mom had by the owner of this face looking out at us. I recognized the narrowed eyes, the swooping eyebrows, the beaked nose, and the arrogant lips drawn back in a smile—recognized them as if I'd somehow always known them.

Here was Lorenzo da Padova, the ancient evil. Laughing at us.

I sucked in my breath and, never taking my eyes from the face on the canvas, turned both water taps on full blast. Lorenzo da Padova's low-pitched chuckle filled the room, even as the paint began dripping down his cheeks.

I somehow heard Fitzgerald Cotton's agonized whisper over the sound of the rushing water. "My poor Pamela! Will you ever be able to forgive me?"

I dumped out every last grain of powdery pigment from the old box, and tossed the paint box into the sink under the flow. Then the laughing, taunting face was fading, and I could see Mom's face there again, underneath.

The luminous hues were changing, growing softer. The shapes and shadows that had formed the portrait of Mom were evaporating as the last powders of ancient pigment were disappearing down the drain under the surge of water.

And then the canvas was blank.

"She's gone!" cried Fitzgerald Cotton, tears of remorse on his cheeks.

I turned off the taps. There was silence, heavy and complete.

"Not gone," I said. *"Safe."*

∾ Chapter 16 ∾

A New Muse

We left Fitzgerald Cotton up in the studio, sitting on the couch with his head in his hands. And although Homer and Betty hadn't wanted to leave him there alone, he insisted they go downstairs.

"I have to think," he told us, drooping down onto the couch and staring at the blank canvas on the easel. "So much to think about—so much..." His voice trailed off. Betty looked worried. We all stood there for a moment or two, watching him, until Mrs. Cotton called us to come down to lunch. "You go," he muttered again. "Please go."

I remembered how weak and fuzzy I'd felt after first traveling back through time to 1926. It was sort of like that now, and I could tell Betty and Homer felt the same. Maybe that's how their uncle Fitzy was feeling, alone up in his studio.

Being touched by magic takes a lot out of you.

"What now?" Homer kept asking in a vague sort of

way as we sat at the lunch table. "What happens next?" But Betty and I had no answer.

"What are you talking about?" Elsie demanded to know.

"You're too young," Homer said importantly. That set Elsie off, of course, and so Betty and I had to sit there listening to them bicker. I slid low in my chair and munched my egg salad sandwich. I still, after all that, didn't have the sketch.

Then Elsie started fretting about how she felt guilty for upsetting dear Uncle Fitzy with the lie about his muse's return. And how poor old Chess was stuck up in his bed because of his fake stomachache. And how Joanna was still out on her date with Mr. Riley.

This last comment made Betty sit up and shake some of the fuzziness out of her head. "Still out?" she asked shrilly. *"Still?"*

"It's not really been that long," I told her. "It just seems that way."

She frowned at me and went out on the front porch to see if her mother was coming. "Not a sign," she reported, coming back to finish her lunch. "How much fun can they be having? As much as we've been having, do you think?"

I'm not sure I'd call what had been happening to us *fun,* but things were sure more interesting here than they'd ever been at home.

After lunch Homer went up to slip his younger brother a sandwich. And when Mrs. Cotton sent us out to do some marketing, as she called grocery shopping, we decided the errand would go more quickly on wheels. We could see Chess watching us from his bedroom window as we strapped on those clunky metal skates (I wore Betty's old ones, the ones she was saving to hand down to Elsie). The skates fastened on to our shoes, and tightened with a funny key. Betty reached for my hand and led me down Lemon Street at top speed.

I felt wind in my face—real wind, not time-traveling wind—and it felt good. Everything suddenly felt great, in fact: the wind in my face, and Betty's hand holding mine, and the way we were clattering along and laughing hilariously and getting looks from some old people out tending their gardens. *Kids* today, you know.

At home in my neighborhood, in my time, there wouldn't have been all those people outside working. There wouldn't have been any parade of roller-skating kids, either, of course.

Homer came clattering up to Betty and me. "Hey, you two," he huffed, trying to keep up. "We need to talk about it! About what happened with Uncle Fitz and the paints—"

Betty turned around. "Will you hush up?" she demanded with a pointed look over at Elsie, racing up behind us. Betty took off her skates and marched into the shop while Homer, Elsie, and I waited outside, whirling as fast as we could around a lamppost. We went so fast I felt a wind again.

Time to fly home, I thought wildly.

"Look!" Elsie cried. "Look up ahead!"

"Hey, is that Mama?" squawked Homer. "And Mr. Riley?"

"Hay is for horses, Homeboy," I shouted. "Can't you keep that in your thick head?" How come I felt so giddy? We watched Mr. Riley's horse and cart up ahead, just turning onto East Main Street, with Mr. Riley and Joanna high on the padded driver's bench.

I went into racing mode. I had energy to burn. I was *surging* with energy.

I skidded to a stop just before plowing into the back of the ice wagon—it was a lot harder to maneuver on metal skates than with my Rollerblades. "Hello, Mrs. Cotton!" I called. "You'll be glad to know that Chester is feeling much better. He's eaten lunch and is doing just fine. And hello, Mr. Riley!" I waved to him as if we were old chums. "I loved the swimming hole! Thanks for recommending it, sir!"

He smiled down at me a little nervously, like he couldn't quite remember who I was or how I knew his name. "Hello, old Nellie," I added to the horse. "Bye, now!"

I had so much energy, I zoomed back to the market at top speed. Betty was strapping on her skates again. She handed me the basket of food to carry, and I felt a sudden stab of sadness at the touch of her hand, and the crazy burst of energy popped like a balloon.

We skated home together, letting Elsie set the pace. Joanna was sitting on the porch with Mrs. Cotton and Chester, who shouted to us that he felt completely well again. Joanna told about her date—*outing*, she called it—with Mr. Riley. They'd gone on a long walk by the water, and he'd told her all about how he loved to fish. Then they ate lunch at the Walnut Inn—no harp player at lunchtime; only dinner, alas—and he told her all about his collection of seashells. Then they'd walked over to Mason Ice, where Mr. Riley worked, and he and Nellie had brought her home in the ice wagon.

"Did he kiss you, Mama?" asked Elsie.

"Hush, child!" exclaimed Mrs. Cotton. "That's not a thing a young girl should be asking."

"Well, did he?" pressed Betty.

Joanna's cheeks turned pink. "Mr. Riley is a gentleman," she told her daughters reprovingly. "A gentleman would never do such a thing on a first date."

"At least you admit it was a date!" said Betty.

"He did not kiss me," Joanna said firmly. "And what's more, I did not want him to." She looked around the table at each of her children. "In fact, I should prefer to kiss Nellie. Especially after he got to talking about shipping the lot of you off to boarding school. I told him nothing doing. And then I told him to bring me home. All right, my lambs?"

"Hooray!" cried Chester. And Elsie and Betty jumped up to hug her.

"I knew it!" Homer laughed his maniacal laugh. "I just knew he'd try the boarding school idea sooner or later."

So that was another mother saved today.

After dinner that night Mr. Cotton carried the card table outside again so we could catch the evening breeze while we tried to fit more pinks and purples of the presidential garden together. There was no sign of Fitzgerald Cotton, of course, and I found myself worrying about the guy. He'd had a rough day, too.

Joanna went upstairs to put Elsie and Chess to bed, and Mrs. Cotton was washing up the dinner dishes. I lay back on the porch swing and let everything sort of wash over me: The warm evening. The scent of mown grass. The clink of ice in Mr. Cotton's lemonade. Betty's grumble when the jigsaw pieces wouldn't fit. And Homer's goblin laugh.

The scents and sounds of 1926.

I didn't know these people very well, and it wasn't like I wanted to live with them forever or anything—but somehow...somehow things were more...interesting. More interesting than with my own family at home. Kids had adventures here, even when the stakes weren't life-or-death. Kids made plans. Kids stuck together. They went places. They let one event lead to another and another. They could just be *spontaneous*. Things were special here.

There, I'd said it.

Did that make me a traitor? I gave myself a little shake like maybe I could shake some sense into myself. I mean, really, what was I thinking of? It was BORING here. I told myself it was very, *very* boring. They lived in the previous century and were technological idiots. They didn't have even such simple things as TV or computer games. They had only the big brown radio that stood in the living room with only, like, two channels—one with rinky-tink–sounding music and one with scratchy voices reading the news: "Hurry out to your neighborhood cinedrome to see *Rin-Tin-Tin,* today's box office hit!" "Flappers swell the ranks of women voters!" "President Coolidge warns that bootlegging is a serious crime and that criminals shall be prosecuted to the full extent of the law..."

"Con?" Homer pushed back his chair and came to sit next to me on the swing, interrupting my thoughts. "Aren't we gonna tell *anybody*?" He kept his voice low so Mr. Cotton wouldn't overhear.

"About *what*?" I couldn't help needling him.

"About the Smiler!" Homer cried.

"Don't," Betty said with a shudder, abandoning the puzzle and coming to sit on my other side. "Don't even mention his name."

"But what happens *now*?" pressed Homer.

"I wish I could see her again." Betty's voice was wistful. "Pammie. Just to be sure she's all right. Just to... visit, you know, the way you've visited us here, Con. And I'd like to see what things are like where you come from. *When* you come from, I mean."

"Me, too," said Homer eagerly. "Will you tell us?"

Before I could answer, we heard the creak of the front screen door opening. *"Sssh!"* Betty warned us.

Joanna and Mrs. Cotton came out onto the porch. Mrs. Cotton lit one of the oil lamps and stood it on the puzzle table. It filled the evening with a soft yellow glow. The two women settled into rocking chairs. Mrs. Cotton worked on something she was knitting in soft green wool.

I watched her fingers moving the needles until they'd almost hypnotized me. Or was it the soft glow of the light that hypnotized me? Or Homer's rhythmic kicking his toe against the floor, sending our swing gently back and forth, back and forth? *What happens now?* Homer had asked.

I had to get that sketch and try to go home, that was what. But here on this porch with these people, the urgency I'd felt since I'd arrived had vanished. I'd known these people only a few days, but leaving wouldn't be easy—maybe because I sensed there'd be no coming back.

When Mom had been away from home a whole year, to us it was only a blink of an eye. We'd never noticed. When I went back, would anyone notice I'd been gone?

When I'd come home from school that day, and Mom was on the couch—with different clothes and different hair and…and feeling different about everything… Would I be different, too, if I ever got back home?

But—*I was already different.*

The thought hit me hard, made me flinch, and sent the porch swing skittering. I was as different as Mom had become, and it had taken only a couple of days—not a year. I mean, I wasn't about to go home and start throwing out the TVs and stuff, but I could sort of see why Mom had. I scrubbed my fingers through my hair, hard. I could almost hear Crystal's derisive voice hissing in my ear: *Traitor!*

The screen door creaked. I looked over, expecting maybe Elsie to be out of bed, trying to creep back out here with us old folks. But no—it was Fitzgerald Cotton himself poking his head out. Everyone noticed at the same time, and sat up suddenly and stopped what they were doing. Betty dropped a puzzle piece. Homer stopped rocking the swing. Mrs. Cotton's fingers on the knitting needles seemed to freeze in midair.

Mr. Cotton cleared his throat. "Fitz, my boy."

"Here, dear," Mrs. Cotton said brightly, struggling out of her rocker. "Sit down right here and let me get you something to drink!"

"Sit over here with me and Con, Uncle Fitzy," invited Homer, scooting to the corner of the swing so there would be room for the artist between us.

"You're good at puzzles, Uncle Fitzy," said Betty with a big smile. "Can you help me—"

"Joanna," Fitzgerald Cotton said slowly. His eyes raked over each of us, coming to rest on Joanna at the puzzle table.

"Fitz!" she said with a sudden glad smile, like maybe she was thinking he meant to share his lottery winnings or something.

She sat him down, acting like this was totally normal for him to be here with his family. "How is your work going these days?"

"Not well at all, I'm afraid."

"Oh, dear, I hope the children have not been pestering you."

"Not at all," he said grandly. "They've been no trouble at all. Very helpful children, actually. For the most part. No, Joanna, my dear. It is not the children's fault I've been deprived of my muse."

"*Ahh,*" she said softly.

"Something to drink, Fitz?" asked Mrs. Cotton eagerly. "A cup of tea? Just tell me what you need."

"No tea, Mama," he said. "What I need is right here—but it isn't tea."

"Perhaps a nice sandwich?" ventured Joanna. "There's leftover meatloaf—"

"I need *you,* Joanna. Upstairs."

"Me?!"

"In the studio."

Of course, I thought.

"How wonderful!" cried Joanna. "Will you paint me?" She pushed back her chair and stood up. She had a great big smile on her face, like maybe she'd applied for the position of New Muse and thought she was about to get the job.

He shot another look around at all of us sitting there, then walked over to me. He fished in his trouser pocket and brought out a folded sheet of white paper. "I found this yesterday—blown under the couch. It's for you, young man. Your train ticket home, perhaps?"

I took the paper and started to unfold it, not sure for a moment what it was, because the sketch as I'd last seen it had been yellowed with age. But sure enough, it was the charcoal sketch, on paper still white. There was Mom, sitting in the grass, smiling up at me and holding out her hand. The paper seemed to pulse in my hand—blown by a strong wind.

I folded the paper closed again—quick—and looked up at him. There was suddenly a huge lump in my throat. "Thank you," I whispered.

"My pleasure," he said gently. "Seems to me you've earned it."

Then Fitzgerald Cotton held open the screen door and beckoned for Joanna. She flashed us all this big smile—quizzical, but triumphant, too, it seemed to me—and went inside. Fitzgerald Cotton looked back—straight at me—and winked.

∽ Chapter 17 ∽

The Souvenir

The screen door closed softly behind them. Homer and Betty leaned toward me excitedly, wanting to see the sketch. But I held it folded on my lap. *My lifeline! My talisman!* I wasn't about to share.

"Well, Mother?" said Mr. Cotton.

"Fitz is coming back to us," replied Mrs. Cotton. She sounded all choked up. "Oh, Edgar, he's coming back."

"Now, we don't know that, Mother," Mr. Cotton said gently.

"I feel sure of it. He came downstairs! It has been ages and ages—ever since Pamela left us. Maybe now—"

"Well, it's a beginning, I'll grant you that," interrupted Mr. Cotton. "But when Fitz gets into one of his black moods, it can last months. Years! You know that."

"He came down," Mrs. Cotton said firmly. She picked up her knitting. "I say that is a very big step. And you know how he's always adored Joanna...Maybe now..." She glanced over at Betty and Homer and me and fell silent.

"Mama was in love with him," said Betty. "I'm sure she was. I thought it would be perfect, after Daddy died, if she and Uncle Fitzy could marry. I mean, it's okay for a woman to marry the brother of her dead husband. Henry the Eighth's first wife, Catherine of Aragon, was married to his older brother, Arthur, first! But then Arthur died before he ever became king...and Catherine married Henry, the younger brother..."

I felt like I was back home with Crystal, with her talk of royalty and weddings. I bet Betty would have been a major Prince William fan, too, if she lived in my time. Must be something about thirteen-year-old girls.

"Don't rush things, Betty, lamb," said her grandmother. But the two of them exchanged pleased looks.

"And he's *so* much better than Mr. Riley," Betty continued. "And you know it's true, Gramma. Who better for Mama than another of your own sons?"

"All in good time," Grandpa murmured. "All in good time."

"Speaking of time," Mrs. Cotton said calmly, "it's almost time for bed. All three of you children. Don't forget, school starts again tomorrow. Joanna will have to take you to get registered, Con. Maybe you can be in Homer's class."

"It would be the cat's pajamas!" cheered Homer, and I had to laugh.

"It would be awesome," I agreed. "I mean, it would be the bee's knees to stay here and be in Homer's class— but I can't."

"You can't? Why not? You won't want to be in Miss

Gruber's class, believe me," said Homer. "Miss Anderson is much nicer and—"

"I mean I won't be staying here." It had hit me, seeing Fitzgerald Cotton trying to get on with his life in a new way, that that's what my mom was free to do now, too. With the paints gone, nothing was holding her to this time anymore—and now that I had the sketch, nothing was holding me.

"I have to leave," I told the Cottons. I smoothed my hand over the folded paper in my lap.

"Dear boy, you're most welcome to make your home with us," Mrs. Cotton said. "An orphan boy like yourself needs a family."

"Thank you," I said.

Mr. Cotton turned puzzled eyes to me. "Where would you rather go, lad?"

"Um, I don't know, really," I said. "I mean, I like it here just fine on Lemon Street."

I could tell Homer was just bursting to talk to me, so I got up and said good night to Mr. and Mrs. Cotton. I went inside, and Homer followed me. Then Betty came in, too, and darted up the stairs in front of us.

We sat on Homer's bed in our bedroom, whispering because Chester was sound asleep. "Are you really going?" Homer asked. "Back wherever Pammie went? Are you going now? Tonight?"

"*Sssh!*" I hissed, looking over at Chess, fast asleep and snoring, on his back in the bed by the window. My head was aching from all the stuff that had happened that day. And I was thinking all sorts of weird stuff, like how the tree in Doug's yard might be a good place to build a fort.... And that real hammers and nails couldn't be too different from the cyber ones I used in the Carpenter Gothic game, the one where you smash the nails as they try to jump out of the wood so the haunted mansion will fall down.... I could take what I'd learned about fort building with Elsie and Homer and Chess home with me. And if Doug and I explored around our neighborhood, we might be able to find some trace of the streams that must still flow underground.

"Let's see that sketch," begged Betty.

"Well, I don't know," I said, holding it tight. I could feel the wind pulsing around me, though neither of the other two seemed to notice. "You can't touch it! Promise me you'll just look."

She and Homer leaned over the sketch. "Be careful!" I yelped, pushing them back. "If you touch it by mistake—and that wind starts blowing—who knows where you'll end up!" *And it's my ticket home.* If one of them disappeared with it, I would be stuck here forever. True, there could be worse places to live—but if there was one thing I'd learned from my time with the Cotton family, it was that family mattered and that home was home.

"Look how Pammie is smiling and holding out her hand," said Betty. "She looks so happy—and so real. Makes you want to touch her, doesn't it?"

In a panic I reached out and picked up the sketch by its corner and folded it securely closed again. The pulse of wind receded.

"Take me with you," murmured Betty.

"*What?*"

"I want to see what it's like in the future!"

"Oh, Betty," I hissed. "You belong *here.*" It sounded hokey, but I knew it was true. "And besides, what if the wind doesn't blow you home with me, but somewhere else? What if it blows you back in time—back to Lorenzo da Padova's time?" I shook my head.

"I don't care," she insisted. "I want to try. I want some adventure! I want to find out that magic is real!"

"Forget it, Betty. Just forget it!" But I didn't know how to fight her if she really meant to come. And maybe it would be cool, after all. She would be a better sister than Crystal, probably.

"*Could* that happen?" demanded Homer. "I mean, going to da Padova's time?" His face looked ashen in the moonlight.

"Who knows?" I said. "Who knows for sure if the sketch will even work again? After all, the old paints are gone. The magic might be over—" I stopped. I knew it wasn't true. I could feel the wind waiting for me.

"And would that be so terrible?" Betty whispered, her eyes bright, challenging me in that way she had. "If you had to stay here with us?"

I grinned at her. "Not *so* terrible at all, if you really want to know the truth." In fact, I was realizing, the only thing wrong with 1926, really, was that my family—okay, and Doug—weren't in it. "It's a pretty nice time to live in."

After a long moment she smiled back at me. "What's it like, then, in your time?"

Whoa. That was a big question. "Well," I said after a moment, "you'll see for yourself, won't you? When you get there someday. You'll be an old lady, of course, but you'll get there." And for a second all the things I'd managed to pick up in my history lessons flashed in my mind—all the troubles Betty would have to live through before she made it to my time. The Great Depression. World War II. Vietnam. Terrorist attacks and...*yikes.*

Something in my face must have worried her, because Betty nudged me. "What's wrong with your time then?" she asked.

I sighed. "There's a lot that's wrong with the future. But there are good things, too. In my time your dad wouldn't have died from pneumonia, probably. There are medicines you've never heard of that can fix tons of things." I hesitated. "There's nothing really wrong with my time—except maybe there's too much going on..."

"Is Pammie happy in your time?" Betty pressed. "Because she could come back here, you know. If she's not happy, I mean..."

I drew in a big breath. "Maybe she wasn't happy," I said. "But she will be." And then I stood up abruptly, the sketch firmly in my hand. "I've got to go. I really do."

Betty said nothing, but her silence took up a lot of space.

I headed out into the hall. Homer trotted at my side. Betty followed more slowly. I went into the girls' bedroom and stood by Elsie's bed. I reached out a finger and touched her silky hair. "Bye, Party Girl," I whispered.

I turned and walked to the end of the hall, with both

of them dogging my steps. I slipped into Mr. and Mrs. Cotton's empty master bedroom. The room was dark, but I could see a pad of paper on the nightstand between the two neatly made beds. I picked up a pencil and wrote in my best handwriting:

Dear Mr. and Mrs. Cotton,

You have been so nice to have me as your guest. I am not really an orphan. I lied about that, although in this time I sort of am an orphan. So it was only half a lie. But I have to go home now. Pamela is my mother. Homer and Betty and their uncle Fitz can tell you all about it.

Thanks again for everything. For talking at meals, for the lemonade and the puzzle on the porch. And everything.

Love, Connor

Homer was reading over my shoulder. "So you're really going?"

I turned and looked at him in the dim room. He was this skinny kid with dark hair slicked back from a center part, and round wire glasses—and the saddest face. A weird thought stabbed me: In my own time Homer would be an old, old man by now. He might even be dead! But if he were still alive, and if I were to look for him...

It was an unsettling thought. I shoved it away. "I'm going," I said.

Ready or not I all but ran up the last flight of steps to the attic studio. Of course, Homer and Betty followed right behind me. I hesitated outside the studio door. I could hear voices murmuring in there. I raised my hand and tapped at the door. The voices stopped.

"Go away!" boomed Fitzgerald Cotton.

"It's me," I said.

"And me," called Homer.

"Me, too," said Betty.

There was silence from inside the studio. I hesitated, then turned the knob and went in, anyway. "I've come to say good-bye," I mumbled, quickly taking in the scene in the studio. I could see why old Fitzy didn't want any interruptions. The room was aglow with soft lamplight. Joanna was curled up on the couch, holding one of those roses. He had a paintbrush in his hand and a canvas on the big easel. There was already a good sketch there in blocks of soft color. Joanna's face was recognizably hers, looking out over the rose with an expression of—a sort of *mischief*. As if she were trying not to burst out laughing at the dumbness of sitting on an artist's couch holding a rose. Her almost smile was what was going to make the painting really good, I thought.

"So you like this one then, boy? Better than the other?"

I nodded. "Much, much better. *This* muse looks like she's having fun."

"Hello, Mama," said Homer, sort of sounding embarrassed.

Joanna laughed and lowered the rose. "Hello, children. I am having fun. I'm delighted to be Fitz's model again. It's been a long time..." Her voice trailed off. She must have been jealous of my mom, I decided. Even though she'd liked her, too.

"So you're leaving us?" asked Fitzgerald Cotton. "Do you have your travel documents in order?" His voice was genial, as if there had never been any trouble between us.

Joanna's smooth forehead creased in a frown. "Now, where in the world would you be going at this time of night? You children should be in bed by now!"

"Homer and Betty will tell you all about it," I said quickly. "But yes, I'm ready." I held up the sketch.

"Ready for what?" asked Joanna. "Connor, may I see that drawing?" She reached for it.

"Careful—don't touch it!" I cried and snatched it back.

Joanna looked astonished and totally confused, poor lady. And it was going to get wilder. But she'd have people to comfort her, I told myself, when things got *really* weird.

"It's a sketch of Pammie, and Pammie's his *mother,* Mama!" said Homer importantly. "And there's more— wait till you hear about the paint box—"

"Hush up, Homer!" said Betty. "Not now!"

I could see Homer was dying to tell the whole story, but Fitzgerald Cotton held up a hand to silence him. Joanna looked confused.

"Wait, all of you. Let's watch now how young Connor is going to take his leave of us." The artist turned to me. "Seeing is believing. That's what magicians rely on, and so do artists. Art creates. So why should we be surprised when sometimes real life comes up with a little magic of its own?" He moved to the small easel and smiled at me. "But before you leave us, I want to give you a souvenir. Show it to your sweet mother, so she'll know what her scamp of a son got up to during his short visit." He turned the easel around. We all stared. It took me a second to realize what I was looking at—then I groaned.

"I look pathetic!"

"It looks just like you," said Betty.

"Oh, Fitzy," said Joanna. "How dreadful of you. Did you really stand there sketching from life while the poor boy was—"

Now Homer was into his maniacal giggle. "He was! He did! He just stood there sketching while Connor was—"

Hanging from the skylight, that's what everybody was trying to say. There I was, in oils, hanging from the studio skylight, my shirt twisted up and my mouth open in a cry for help. It should have been a pitiful thing to see, but it had me cracking up, and even the artist himself couldn't suppress a little twitch of the lips.

"It's so cool!" I said. "I mean, it's the bee's knees. I'll keep it forever," I added. "Unless somebody pays us a fortune and sticks it in an art museum with your other paintings."

Fitzgerald Cotton shook his head. "Now you are pulling my leg again."

I realized the man really didn't get that he was going to become famous and have books written about him and have his work hanging in museums all around the world. "I'm totally serious," I told him. "You're a famous man. I read all about you in an art book—" But then I broke off, remembering what I'd read. I didn't want to tell him any more—about how he never painted again after his muse left him. About how he committed suicide out of his despair…

But now he pulled Joanna off the couch and danced her around the room. "Hear that?" he crowed. "A famous man!"

Then Fitzgerald Cotton lifted the painting of me and the skylight carefully off the easel. "Now, mind that the paint's still wet," he said. "Won't be dry for a week. Hold it here, by the edge of the wood frame. And take this, too. For your mother. Proof that I never meant to hurt her." He went to the locked cupboard and drew out the ancient paint box. The dark box was dry again after its shower in the sink. Even empty, blackened with age, metal clasp broken, the box seemed to hold secrets. I held it gingerly, as if it might bite.

"I wish you'd be here for school tomorrow, Connor," said Homer in a forlorn voice. "You'd like Miss Anderson. She's the cat's meow."

I looked at Homer and felt again a little stab of something—pity? amazement?—to think that he was all grown-up and old, maybe even dead, in my time, but here he was just a kid, just my age, with the whole rest of his life before him, with all the time in the world. I looked over at Betty and wondered who she would become. Made me think how all our lives go by pretty fast.

How it's important not to waste them. I decided I would look for them both. Search the Web. Send them an e-mail if they were still around. But if they weren't . . .

I set the painting and paint box carefully on the floor.

"Here, Homeboy," I said, rooting around in my pants pocket. "I'll tell you what's really the cat's meow." I tossed him the key chain. I could get Doug another, *no problemo*. "It's a *Star Wars* key chain. A lucky charm. Just hold it for a minute—see what happens?"

Homer stared down at the little Death Star like it was magic in his hand and then sucked in his breath when his palm warmed it enough to make it flash its red light.

I had nothing for Betty. I didn't want things to get gooey, but I was just standing there, just looking at her, and wishing I had something to give her. She reached out her hands suddenly to clasp mine. Her hands were warm, and then our arms were around each other for a quick hug, and that was a little bit of magic, too.

Finally I stepped away from her and looked around at them all one more time. "And now for my next act—" I said softly. Homer with the flashing key chain. Fitzy standing by his easel. Joanna on the couch in front of me. Betty with her arms folded tightly across her body as if in defiance of magic.

I sat gingerly on the arm of the couch. I held the painting of the skylight by the canvas's wooden frame. I tucked the ancient paint box under my arm. Then I smoothed the folded sketch open on my knee. I took a deep breath and looked up at the skylight, a moonlit square on the ceiling.

"Good-bye," I whispered to everybody, to the room, to 1926, and I slowly rubbed my finger across Mom's outstretched hand.

The wind started blowing just as strong as before, but this time I was ready for it. I braced myself, clutching the painting and the box as tightly as I could. I opened my mouth to say something memorable or witty or special enough so that the Cottons would always remember me by it, but the wind was too strong. I couldn't talk, and I couldn't see, and I couldn't hear. I could barely breathe. I could barely think. I was falling now, falling— and I forgot where I was going or what I had been doing or even who I was. The icy wind swept me up and around, inside out—and away.

Chapter 18

Ticket Home

I *must have been sick for a long time,* I was thinking as I tried to open my eyes. *Maybe influenza or scarlet fever or something.* I felt so heavy and dizzy. I must have fallen out of bed onto the floor. The carpet scratched my cheek, and I could barely lift my head. There was something poking into my side, and I tried to shift away. A dark wooden box—

I struggled to sit up, and there I was in my bedroom, and my mom was sitting on my bed staring down at me.

"Connor!"

"Mom!"

She was on the floor next to me in a flash, and all over me with big hugs and kisses. "You're home! You're back!"

I couldn't stop hugging her. I felt I was waking from a dream. I didn't know what was real, and I drew back to stare right into her eyes. "Mom," I breathed. "Were you really, truly *there*? Were you Fitzgerald Cotton's *muse*?"

Mom reached out her hand. She touched my cheek very softly. "My own, dear Connor," she said. "I missed you very much while I was gone."

"And now *I've* been gone," I said, and it all came flooding back to me.

"Yes," she said. "How long were you there?"

"Just a few days," I said. "How long did it seem?"

She sat back and looked at me. "I'm not sure. I've been sitting here—frozen, I think. You know. But some part of me was terribly aware that you were gone. That you'd gone back, for my sake. The wind started blowing—"

"You could feel it, too?"

"Oh yes, it was that same cold wind I remember so well. And then you sort of just...faded. Like in a film. *Fade to black.*"

It was creepy hearing her describe it.

Dad and Crystal raced into the room just then and stopped dead in their tracks when they saw me and Mom talking together. "The ambulance is on its way, Pam!" cried Dad, falling to his knees on the floor beside us. He took Mom into his arms and pressed his head to her chest, listening to her heartbeat. He fumbled with her wrist, searching out her pulse.

"I'm all right, Grant. I'm fine now," Mom said, her eyes meeting mine over Dad's bowed head.

Crystal was staring at me. "Con?" she asked. "What's happened? How did you snap Mom out of it this time?" She shook her head. "Wait a sec—where'd you get the weird clothes?"

I shrugged, completely without words just then to tell her anything. In my mind I was still with the Cottons, up in the studio. I could see them standing there, staring at the empty spot where I'd been sitting....

We could all hear the wail of an ambulance coming down our street.

"I'd better go tell them you're okay," Dad said. "If you really are okay, Pam. But I think you ought to let them look at you. This is happening a lot. It's not normal."

"It won't happen again," I said. I sank back against the bed, feeling totally wiped out. Maybe I was the one who needed the ambulance.

Mom ran her fingers through my hair. "My darling boy," she said, even though Crystal was right there, listening to every word. "I was never so frightened as when I saw you disappear—and never so relieved as when I saw you come back."

"Tell me what happened," I said weakly. "Tell me what you saw."

"Tell me, too," said Crystal. "Either I've entered the Twilight Zone, or else I've missed something *big*. Hey, no fair."

"Well, I sat there for a few seconds," Mom said, ignoring Crystal. She ran her fingers through her short, bobbed hair. "The wind stopped. Everything seemed very quiet. I tried to imagine you landing somewhere at the Cottons. I couldn't imagine how you would manage. I felt so afraid for you—meeting them, meeting Fitz—" She stopped. "Did you? Did you meet Fitz?" She pointed at the painting she'd picked up and stood against the dresser before I'd opened my eyes. "You must have met him. Did he paint this? Connor, what were you *doing*?"

"Oh, just trying to rescue *you*," I said. I tried to stand up. Mom had to help me. I felt so shaky. I staggered over to the bed and sank down on it. The clock by my bed said 7:30.

Crystal let out a shriek. She hadn't noticed the painting till then. "Connor," she cried, "something really did happen to you, didn't it! In just those few minutes, while Dad and I were calling the ambulance?" She reached out for the painting. "But this is impossible."

"Yup—but watch it," I warned her. "It may be impossible, but the paint's still wet—"

"And what's that you're holding?" asked Mom.

I held it out to her. "His paint box. Not Fitz's—it belonged to a man who died back in 1479. His name was Lorenzo da Padova, but he can't hurt you now."

She took it gingerly. "Oh, Connor, tell me everything."

We had to wait until the paramedics examined her and pronounced her fit and fine, and said if she had any other seizures, she should not hesitate to call them again. Best to make an appointment to see her own doctor first thing tomorrow. "Yes, I'll do that," she said, but I knew she wouldn't.

Dad had to go downstairs with them to see them off, but he looked worriedly over his shoulder at us as he left the room. *Don't worry,* I thought. *We'll be here.*

Mom and I just sat there on my bed. Crystal sat on the floor. We all knew we were waiting for Dad to come back. I stared around my bedroom like I hadn't seen it in a year. I felt like I'd been away for a very, very long time—longer than a few days. And I had such a strange feeling inside. Like something was missing. Like—where was Betty now? I could imagine her sitting with Homer, trying to tell their mother about the magic. I could imagine Elsie and Chess fast asleep in their rooms...in their house that once stood exactly where our house stood now. Maybe this bedroom was in the same space as one of theirs had been. I tried to orient myself: If this was the boys' room, then Homer's bed would be over by the window, Chester's near the door. My camp bed set up over there, where my computer desk stood...

My room seemed too bright, somehow. Too cluttered. I didn't like the spaceship bed as much as I had before I'd gone to the Cottons...although I knew Homer would love it. I wished I could give it to him and have the narrow little camp bed back.

"It's hard, isn't it?" Mom said, watching me closely. "Hard to come back."

She knew. Thank goodness someone knew how I felt. But poor Mom—how hard it must have been for her after more than a whole year away, with all of us thinking she was so weird, and getting all mad at her about the TVs and stuff. I gave her a grateful smile.

We heard Dad's footsteps running up the stairs, and then there he was again. He sat on the floor with Crystal.

"Now tell me what is going on," he said. "Everything."

And then I started to tell them all that had happened from the moment I found myself on the floor in Fitzgerald Cotton's studio. But Crystal kept interrupting and making noises of total disbelief like, *Oh, yeah, riiiight,* until Dad shushed her.

"I don't believe a word of this, either," he said. "But then again, how can I *not* believe? Look at Con's clothes! And you saw what was happening to Mom! And now here's this painting—out of thin air!"

So Crystal finally sat back, leaned against the wall, and shut up.

I told them about the ancient paints and rumors of poison and the madman whose nickname was the Smiler. I told them everything I could remember—even about Mr. Riley and the plan to paint a pus-filled rash, and about flooding the kitchen and trying to climb through the skylight. I told them about roller-skating and swimming and building the fort and doing the puzzle.

"And you liked Mabel and Edgar?" Mom asked. "And what about Joanna?"

I said they were all wonderful, and they were all doing fine—and that maybe now Joanna was doing even finer than before. "I think she was in love with Fitz," I said. "And didn't dare tell him. And he was in such a black mood after you left, he couldn't even see her. But now..." and I told them about Joanna's sitting with the rose for her portrait, and how it was coming out so much better than the portrait he was trying to do of Mom. I told Mom about the horrible painting of her frozen, the way I'd left her, and how it seemed to turn uglier and more agonized every minute.

"Poor Fitzy was obsessed," Mom said. "But more

than that—he was possessed. I understand it now. And it makes sense of why I stayed so long. As long as he was painting me, I was compelled to stay. But, oh, how I missed you and Crystal."

She didn't forget us! She had missed us! "And Dad?" I said softly.

"Even Dad," Mom said, glancing over at him. "Yes, I missed you, Grant darling. Things weren't working out very well for us before I…was taken. I had even talked about wanting a divorce. But being away from home gave me a new perspective on what's important." She reached down and took Dad's hand.

He pressed her fingers to his lips. I wasn't used to seeing my parents touch, but it made me feel warm and happy. "Tell me how it happened, Pam," Dad urged. "The magic."

Mom's eyes grew distant. "I was on my way through the living room, heading for the door, when my cell phone rang in my briefcase. I dumped my purse on the coffee table and opened my briefcase to get the phone, and somehow I knocked the pile of art books the decorator had put there right off the table. My boss was on the phone, reminding me to be early for a meeting. So I was in a hurry, and I scooped the books back up as fast as I could, and a sketch flew out of one and landed on the floor in front of me. The person in the old sketch looked so much like me, I was amazed! I had to stop and pick it up." She took a deep breath. "And the way the hand is reaching out in the sketch—it just makes you want to touch it, doesn't it?"

I nodded. "And so you did."

"Yes," Mom said slowly. "I rubbed my finger over the drawing...And there was somehow a freezing wind in our living room, and I felt I was being blown around and around in a sort of whirl...Connor, you must know exactly how strange it was. The strangest feeling I've ever had in my life. I thought for a second I was fainting, or that I was dying, I don't know...And I just had to close my eyes and sink down onto the floor. But after a few seconds when I stopped feeling so dizzy, I realized that the stuff under me wasn't *rug* anymore—but *grass*." Mom looked at Dad wonderingly. "Grant, it was grass, and somehow I was outside, and not in the living room anymore. I thought for a second I must have been blown out into our yard without realizing it, but when I looked up, I was in a garden, and there was a man sitting a few yards away, waving a piece of paper at me. 'The spitting image,' he kept saying. 'The spitting image!'"

"It was this guy you're talking about—Fitzgerald Cotton?" asked Crystal.

"Indeed it was," replied Mom.

"And you went home with him?" Crystal shook her head in disgust. "Mom, after all you tell us about staying away from strangers?"

"It didn't seem strange, dear, and I was dreadfully confused." Mom shook her head, the soft curls bobbing against her cheeks. "The whole time I was there I felt I was under a spell. Or in a daze. It's hard to describe. I just enjoyed the quiet pace of life there with the Cotton family. Mornings in the studio, afternoons with Joanna and Mabel, cooking and cleaning, sewing and talking together. Playing with the children. Taking long walks around the beautiful countryside...It looked so different around here then, Crystal, you can't imagine. The same hills, of course, but groves of lemon trees in the valley, and walnut trees and almond trees...No freeway at all! No big roads...Only Mount Diablo looked the same."

"I know," I murmured, remembering how glad I'd been to see it.

She heaved a big sigh. "Anyway, it wasn't until Fitz went away for a few days to San Francisco to buy more supplies—you know, paints and canvases, artist things— and wasn't painting me, that I started to remember my family and the life I'd left behind. When he wasn't painting me, my memory returned, and I remembered you kids and Dad and everything! I thought, *I've got to get home again!* I knew I couldn't tell all of you what had happened to me, because who would believe it? I wasn't even sure how I'd arrived there in the first place. I went over that morning in my mind, tried to remember what exactly had happened. Getting ready for work...answering the phone...knocking the books on the floor... finding the sketch...And that's when it hit me. The sketch!"

"It took me a little while to think of it, too, Mom," I told her.

Mom ran her fingers over my face. "Thank goodness you figured things out, Connor. It makes me shiver to think of you there, all alone."

I knew what she meant, though I'd hardly been alone for even a second.

"Then Fitz got sick," Mom continued. "Influenza. Very serious in those days. So he couldn't paint for weeks and weeks. During that time I regained all my strong memories of home again *and* searched his studio for the sketch he'd done of me—this one." She fingered the edge of the sketch. "I held the sketch and rubbed it—and I was gone. I didn't even say good-bye."

I let out a long breath. I hadn't even realized I'd been holding it in. "Well, he sure went crazy missing you, once he realized his muse was gone."

Mom patted my knee. Then she reached across me for the big art book. "Let's see what this book says about Fitzy's post-muse period."

"I already read it, Mom," I told her. "That section called the Dark Years—it was terrible. And it led directly to his suicide."

"No—look here!" cried Mom, and she turned the book so I could see the page.

. . . Fitzgerald Cotton's painting sprang to life in 1925 and lasted until 1926 with a whole new style and vibrancy, and his unnamed muse appears in every one of the paintings from this period.

After a year, Cotton's muse disappeared as suddenly as she'd appeared. Cotton's painting style changed again, growing dark and sinister for a brief time. But soon the cheerful vibrancy of the muse

period returned to Cotton's work in full force, fea-
turing the woman he referred to as his New Muse.
In 1927 he married this new muse, his sister-in-
law, Joanna—widow of his beloved brother, Homer.
Joanna and her four children (Elizabeth, Homer Jr.,
Elsa May, and Chester) became the new subject mat-
ter for Cotton's work over the next ten years. To-
gether, Cotton and Joanna had two more children, a
son, Connor, and a daughter, Pamela, who also star
in many of his paintings from the 1930s–1950s.

"Connor and Pamela!" I exclaimed. "Look here,
Mom, he named his kids after us!"

After his family was grown, Cotton and his wife
lived abroad in their later years, during which he
painted his most famous Night City scenes in towns
and cities and villages all across Europe and Asia.
   Fitzgerald Cotton's work depicted both ordinary
family life and the lives of extraordinary people all
around the globe, but in all his work, with the ex-
ception of the short-lived Dark Years period, Cotton
was able to convey the beauty, love, and humor of
the people and situations around him with almost
photographic detail. His paintings now hang in the
permanent collection of the San Francisco Museum
of Modern Art, the Tate Gallery in London, the Ac-
ademia in Rome, among others, and in private col-
lections worldwide.

His death, in 1978, at age ninety-five, marked the end of a long and glorious career.

I looked up at my mom. There was this huge lump in my throat, like I was going to cry or something. But why would I burst out bawling now, when I hadn't shed a single tear throughout my whole big adventure? "He didn't die," I said, and I could hear the wonder in my voice. "I mean, he's dead now, but he was an *old* guy. He *didn't* commit suicide!"

"No," she agreed, and I saw she was crying, too. "Hats off to you, Connor, my brave boy. You saved him. You saved *us.*"

Dad and Crystal were reaching for the book. "Go on and read it," I said, wiping my cheeks. I glanced at Mom, who returned my watery little smile. "It's the very best bedtime story."

Chapter 19 ⚬

What's Right with This Picture?

They read the book. Crystal twirled her hair round and round her finger while she read, then rolled her eyes at me. Dad just looked sort of stunned, as if his whole family was cracking up right before his very eyes and he didn't have a clue what to do about it. He could have us all committed, I supposed, but then he'd be lonely with just Ashleigh. So he sort of decided to believe us. But you could see he didn't like it one bit.

But what he did like—what I think we all liked— were the little changes that happened in our family. Mom was home a lot more. Dad put his foot down at work and said no more weekend meetings; he had a family to raise. Crystal cut out the piano lessons she was sick of, and I stopped gymnastics. Hanging from that skylight, I'd lost my head for heights.

We said enough was enough, and there wasn't time for everything.

We packed up my *Star Wars* furniture and sent it to

my cousin Brad, in Seattle. He's only seven and is as much a Luke Skywalker fan as I ever was, maybe even more. I got new furniture—plain maple wood bunk beds and matching maple dresser and desk. All very simple and quiet and somehow just nice. I could imagine Homer sleeping in the bottom bunk (I'd nabbed the top one, of course). Sometimes I'd whisper to him at night. *Hey, Homeboy!*

Once I looked in the phone book under COTTON: The only listing was for a **Cotton, Elizabeth** over in San Francisco. That might be Betty. But maybe not. If it *was* Betty, she would be old now—old enough to be my grandmother. When I closed my eyes I could see her perfectly as she was in 1926—tall and thin, with that shiny brown bob of hair and those challenging eyes. Easier just to remember her that way, maybe...but I thought I probably would phone her, once I got my nerve up. "*Hey,* there, Betty old girl," I'd say. Would she know it was me, after so long?

Fitzgerald Cotton's painting now hung in a frame above my bed. The painting had gotten a little smudged at one edge during my—uh—travels. But the frame hid the smudged part. I'd given the ancient wooden paint box to Mom, who displayed it front and center on our mantel in the living room. "Powerful statement," said Mom's decorator when she saw it. "You're learning."

Mom brought back one TV from the storage center where she'd taken everything. She hooked up two computers. I think she donated the pagers and cell phones and everything else to charity. I hardly noticed.

We didn't tell our story to anyone outside the family, not even to Ashleigh or Doug. It's one of those things that happens that you just know won't sound so good in the telling. It's better kept as a memory. But some things, I decided, were nicer *not* kept as memories. Some things you just wanted to be *real*.

Like: "Mom, know what?" I asked at dinner not long after all this happened to us. "I think we should build a front porch on to our house."

"What for?" asked Crystal suspiciously.

I looked at her and couldn't help wishing for the zillionth time that it could be Betty sitting there instead. "Porches are good," I said.

"For drinking lemonade," Mom added with a smile.

"And for working on jigsaw puzzles," I said. "One of the finer things in life."

Dad and Crystal looked at each other and rolled their eyes. They were slowly getting used to us. I was still getting used to us, too. The Rigoletti-Chase family connected in ways none of us could guess to how many other people? And in what surprising ways?

"A front porch is a fine idea, Connor," Mom said. "And jigsaw puzzles, too. They're the bee's knees."

I grinned at her. "Hotsy-totsy, even." And there around the dinner table, as we laughed together, I saw my life suddenly stretching out before me—a life at least as long as Fitzgerald Cotton's had been, and maybe even longer. It was going to be filled with things like family dinners and front porches and glasses of lemonade and jigsaw puzzles and books at bedtime and roller-skating all over town. There were going to be tree forts and swimming holes...and lots of traveling—starting with Italy. Maybe I'd even try my hand at painting. There were going to be big adventures, and—oh, my life was going to be good.

Did I say plain old *good*? Hey—my life was going to be the cat's pajamas.